When She's Bad, I'm Badder: 2

Jiao & Dreek, A Crazy Love Story

Tina J

Copyright 2017

This novel is a work of fiction. Any resemblances to actual events, real people, living or dead, organizations, establishments or locales are products of the author's imagination. Other names, characters, places, and incidents are used fictionally.

Because of the dynamic nature of the Internet, any web address or links contained in this book may have changed since publication, and may no longer be valid.

More Books by Tina J

A Thin Line Between Me & My Thug 1-2
I Got Luv for My Shawty 1-2
Kharis and Caleb: A Different kind of Love 1-2
Loving You is a Battle 1-3
Violet and the Connect 1-3
You Complete Me
Love Will Lead You Back
This Thing Called Love
Are We in This Together 1-3
Shawty Down to Ride For a Boss 1-3
When a Boss Falls in Love 1-3
Let Me Be The One 1-2
We Got That Forever Love
Ain't No Savage Like The One I got 1-2
A Queen & Hustla 1-2 (collab)
Thirsty for a Bad Boy 1-2
Hasaan and Serena: An Unforgettable Love 1-2
We Both End Up With Scars
Are We in this Together 1-3
Caught up Luvin a beast 1-3
A Street King & his Shawty 1-2
I Fell for the Wrong Bad Boy 1-2 (collab)
Addicted to Loving a Boss 1-3
I need that Gangsta Love 1-2 (collab)
Still Luvin' a Beast 1-2
I Wanna Love You 1-2
When She's Bad, I'm Badder 1-3

Jiao

No, no, no, no, no. It can't be the same guy. I killed him three years ago but how ironic is it for him to be called the same name? How do they know him? Does Dreek know what he did to my mom? I stood in the bathroom staring in the mirror replaying what happened that dreadful night.

"Jiao, I need you."

"Mommy what's wrong?" I started panicking right away.

"Meet me at the Double Tree Hotel, room 236. Please hurry."

I made a quick detour and floored it all the way there. I ran two red lights and almost hit a woman and a baby trying to make it to my mom. I hopped out the car in front of the hotel and ran in. I didn't care that my car was still running and all my personal belongings were in there. My mom needed me and that was more important.

I pressed the elevator but it didn't come quick enough so I looked around for the stairwell. I took the steps two at a time and opened the door to the floor. I ran into some guy who seemed to be panicking himself. He stared straight into my eyes and I noticed he had a big tattoo on the side of his neck that read Bash. I kept running until I got to the door and saw it was opened.

I yelled out for my mom and when I found her I dropped to my knees and grabbed my phone. I screamed to the 911 dispatcher and told them to hurry up. I grabbed my moms' hands and told her to stay awake but I felt her hands becoming cold. I put her head on my lap and threw a blanket around her to stay warm.

"I thought he loved me the way I loved him. Jiao, take care of yourself and be careful of who you fall in love with. I love you." Were the last words she said before taking her last breath. Her hand fell out of mine and I let out a scream. I stayed in the room for hours after they took my mom.

"What happened to you J? Why do you have blood on you? Are you ok?"

My dad questioned when I stepped in the house. That's when I realized I never called him. I fell into his arms and cried my eyes out. I felt his tears hitting my head too. Who would want to hurt my mom? She was the nicest person ever and its not because she's my mom. Everyone loved her. My mom was like a socialite and anytime there was an event she was always invited. Her death was the worst thing to ever happen to me.

After the shenanigans at the funeral, I began my searched for the guy I saw leaving the hotel the night my mom was murdered. I spoke to my dad about the information I had and he agreed it was something I needed to do.

See, my dad taught me all types of martial arts. I was deadly to anyone on the streets and often did a few hits for Sommer's dad. I never told her because she would kill me. Him and my dad were cool and they both knew I would go undetected getting to people.

I may be small but they say big things come in small packages. The only reason I couldn't beat Dreek is because his ass always knew when I was about to do something.

6

Anyway, I went on Facebook and typed in Bash and hundreds popped up. I narrowed it to my area and it was still too many. I ended up going to bars everyday hoping to run into him. I didn't ask anyone about him because it would be too suspicious.

I had finally given up on the search and was about to leave when he popped up. He was with a bunch of guys who looked liked they were celebrating. I noticed the tattoo on the side of his neck.

I stayed in the background watching him. It took him a while to leave but when he started giving people a dap and announcing he was leaving that was my chance. I ran out the bar and hid around the back. He came out with another guy. I didn't think I would be able to get him but at least I knew where he hung.

Low and behold the other guy left him outside for a minute, which gave me the time to run up on him. He didn't even flinched when he heard my gun cock. It wasn't until I shot him in the stomach that he knew it wasn't a game. I made sure to let him see me after I let one off in his chest. I wanted badly

7

to kill him but someone came out yelling his name. I never saw the guy and ran to my car.

I went to China for three years after the shooting because my father said he found out who the guy was and he had ties to the new connect. Whoever the new connect was went on a rampage looking for the person who shot his brother, which was me. I never knew who he was speaking of but now that I'm here, its it safe to say they're related? I walked out the bathroom and ran straight into him.

"Who knew the bitch I've been looking for is affiliated with my family somehow?" I tried to move past him but he stood in front of me.

"Tell me right now why I shouldn't fucking kill you." He had me up against the wall with his hands around my throat. I gave him my famous death kick and he dropped me. I landed on my feet and was getting ready to hit him with one of my deadly moves. I heard a gun cock and my hands went in the air.

"I thought you'd see it my way."

"Bash, why the fuck you got a gun on the back of her head?" I heard Percy say.

"Go get my brother. I think he needs to hear this shit."

"Yo, Dreek. You need to get out here." I heard Percy yell. I guess he didn't trust Bash to leave me alone with him.

"Dreek is your brother?" He had the evilest grin on his face.

"Yup. Same mother and father. What do you think he'll say when he finds out about what went down between us?"

"What went down between the two of you?" Dreek said and I put my head down.

"Oh hell no. Don't tell me you fucked my brother."

"Dreek let me explain."

"Bash, please don't make me." I loved Dreek but I know him finding out is going to tear us apart.

"I'm not telling him shit. Bitch, this is your problem. I want to see his face when you tell him."

"Dreek, what's going on?" I looked and Queenie was coming out. I felt my hair being yanked and a gun under my chin.

"Did you fuck my brother?" I started crying.

"Stop Dreek."

9

"I thought you were a virgin but I guess not."

"Yo, Dreek. Listen to what she has to say. You're jumping to conclusions." Percy tried to keep him calm. He tossed me against the wall and kept the gun in the same spot.

"Open your fucking mouth and tell me. I swear if its some foul shit, I'll kill you right here, go back to my mothers party and pretend I didn't know you." Bash had a big ass grin on his face.

"Dreek let her go. I can't have our baby and you're in jail for killing her." Queenie yelled out and he slowly let me go.

"Who you pregnant by?" He asked and I felt his grip loosening up." Percy gave me a look and told me to be still.

"The night we went out to eat, we had sex all over the house. Remember you didn't want to use a condom." At that exact moment I found myself crying harder. I knew he'd be hurt when he found out I shot his brother but to hear he got her pregnant, broke my heart.

"WHAT THE FUCK QUEENIE? YOU KNOW I DON'T WANT ANY KIDS BY YOU."

"You most likely made me lose the one in my stomach so be happy one of us will have your baby." He turned around and looked at me. I used the bathroom on myself but I wanted him to think I lost the baby. After today, I wanted no parts of him. If he thinks I lost it and I made it out of here alive, I swear I won't return.

"Jiao, I'm sorry. Fuck! Are you ok?" He had a sad look on his face and came towards me. I backed away.

"Stay away from me Dreek."

"Jiao, I just told you I loved you."

"And you held a gun to me and treated me like shit, knowing I just told you about my pregnancy." I wiped my eyes.

"I thought you slept with my brother. I fucked up."

"It wouldn't work anyway." I started moving away from him.

"You don't know that."

"Yes I do. I'm the one who tried to kill your brother."

"Come again." Percy stared at me and Queenie had her hand covering her mouth.

"I SHOT YOUR FUCKING BROTHER AND I SWEAR IF I HAD A GUN IN MY HANDS RIGHT NOW, I'D BLOW HIS FUCKING BRAINS OUT IN FRONT OF YOU. HE DOESN'T DESERVE TO LIVE AFTER WHAT HE DID." I went running out the hall.

POW! POW!

I felt the burning sensation but I refused to stop running. I made it to my car and realized I left the fucking keys inside. I hit my head on the steering wheel and kept banging it over and over. How did I let me life get this bad?

KNOCK KNOCK! I looked up and sucked my teeth.

"Let's go. He's trying to break free from them. Its in your best interest to come with me." I didn't ask any questions and prayed I wouldn't die tonight. A few minutes later, I passed out.

"Tell me what happened right now before I kill you." I couldn't see the person and the voice was unrecognizable.

"Kill me then. I'm over all of this. I miss my mom and I'm ready to be with her."

"Your wish is my command."

Lord forgive me for my sins. I closed my eyes and prepared myself for the fate I was about to receive.

Dreek

"Calm down Dreek. She's gone." I heard Percy saying in my ear. Him and Robert were struggling to hold and keep me from chasing Jiao. My brother stood there shaking his head and Queenie had a smirk on her face. I'm sure she was in her glory, seeing what went down. I should choke the shit out of her, just because.

"What is going on out here?" My mom shouted. No one opened their mouth. I told the guys to let me go.

"Daddy, where's Jiao? I wanted her to dance with me." I didn't realize Dree came out here. I kneeled down to her. She was upset and I hated to see her like this.

"She left." I refused to speak bad on Jiao because my daughter loved her and I didn't want to take the image away.

"Where did she go? She promised me a dance." I saw her eyes watering.

"Dree, Jiao had to leave because she did something bad to your uncle. Daddy almost.-"

"Yo, shut the fuck up."

"Dreek there's no need to sugar coat what the Chinese girl did." Queenie said getting on my nerves. I walked up on her and she backed up against the wall. I felt someone trying to pull me away.

"Don't call her the Chinese girl when you're well aware of her name. Second... it's not your place to tell my daughter shit."

"I'm sorry Dreek. It's just she caused all this and you're still taking up for her." The jealousy she displayed on her face was clear as day and heard through her voice. I moved away from her and grabbed my daughters' hand.

"Dreek and Bash. I'm not going to ask again. What is going on?" My mom stood waiting for an answer.

"Let's talk about it later. It's your birthday and you still haven't opened your gifts." Bash escorted her back in the hall.

"Daddy, whatever Jiao did, you have to forgive her. She loves us and I'm sure it was an accident."

I stopped and stared at Dree. She was innocent in all of this. I thought about what she said and I agree; Jiao does love both of us. The only thing is, I confessed my feelings to her and even broke up with Queenie, just to find out she almost murdered my brother. Then she wished death on him again and that didn't sit right with me.

I'm not sure I can forgive her but then again, I need to know why she did it. I know Bash isn't perfect but I never thought someone would want him dead. What made her say he deserved it? Did they know each other prior to her shooting him?

We made our way in the hall and sat down. My mom called Dree up to help open her gifts but she wouldn't leave my side. I saw her playing on a phone and noticed it was Jiao's.

The keys to her car were there too. She handed me the phone and I opened it up. There were photos of us in Aspen, some at her house, in the bed and she caught one of me in the shower. It was only my top half but it was a nice shot.

"I told you she loves you." Dree was over my shoulder looking.

I probably shouldn't have looked but curiosity got the best of me. I went through the text messages and most of them were from me, Sommer, Robert and she had a few saved. I opened the saved ones and saw tons of threatening messages. Whoever the person is, had been watching her. The shit had me wondering what the hell was going on.

"You good." Percy asked.

"Yea. Come outside with me right quick. Dree go with nana. I'll be outside for a minute with uncle Percy." She did like I asked and we went out the door.

"What exactly are we looking for?" Percy asked as we went through Jiao's car.

I don't know but something ain't right. She's been getting messages from someone who's watching her. Wait! Where is she? If her car is here, how did she bounce?" I glanced around the parking lot and blew my breath when I saw blood on the ground.

"FUCKKKKKKKK!" I yelled out remembering she was pregnant and shot at. I can't say for sure she was hit because she's not here.

"She must've been hit." Percy pointed to the ground.

"Damn. Do you think she lost the baby?"

"She said it inside when Queenie mentioned hers."

"Oh shit. What are you going to do now? You know Queenie is stuck in your life forever now." I closed the door to Jiao's car and asked him to keep an eye on Dree.

I needed to run by Jiao's house. He nodded and I jumped in my car and drove straight there. I had no key so I kicked it open. In one sense, I wanted her to be there so I could ask her questions but in another, I'm not sure I wouldn't kill her.

I searched through the house and found nothing. I was on my way out and noticed an envelope on the table addressed to me. She was sending it to my mother's address but why mail me something when she could have told me? I opened it up and got a little teary-eyed reading it.

Dear Andreek,

The reason I'm writing this is because we can never get a moment alone without interruptions. I want you to understand why I'm leaving." I looked around the house. *Did she come home and write this?*

Three years ago, my mom was murdered in a hotel and a guy named Bash was the one leaving when I arrived. Granted, I didn't see him actually pull the trigger but he had

19

panic on his face as he ran past me. At first, I didn't know how to find him but after searching, fate led me straight to him. Unfortunately, I killed him to avenge my mother's death and I'm so sorry for taking him away from his family but my mom was taken from me too. There are no winners in this situation and after reading this, I'm sure you'll hate me for leaving but its something I'll have to live with.

I need you to believe me when I say, we met by pure coincidence but I don't regret anything. I love your daughter as if she were my own and you have become the love of my life. This baby I'm carrying is a gift from you and God and I'm sorry for not telling you sooner. Yes, I could have but I didn't want to cause conflict in your life. You were struggling with your feelings and I didn't want to cause more confusion.

There's nothing I wouldn't do for you or Dree but I also know the temper you have. By the time you get this, I won't be around. I can't live in fear from you and just so you know, our baby will always be protected. I love you more than you know and I hope one day you can forgive me and if not, I understand. Take care Andreek and know that you'll always be in my heart and your son's. Yes, it's a boy, I found out yesterday, which is why I called. Take care of Dree and tell her I miss her already.

Always and Forever,

Jiao

"Fuck!"

"What's up yo?" I heard and looked up to see Percy. I stood and handed him the letter.

"Damn bro."

"I know. I thought she slept with him."

"But why, when you knew she was a virgin."

"Man, I don't even know. Jiao has a way of making me crazy and the thought of a man touching her makes me cringe. I don't understand why Bash would kill her mom though."

"It's obvious you have to talk to him. There's some things he's been keeping from you too."

"I will but she's having my son yo. I'm not going to see him born. What if she lost him? What if she's dead? I fucked up." I said and thought about all the differences I noticed in her body. How did I not know she was pregnant? Why didn't she just tell me?

"Where you going now?"

"Home. I have some shit I need to figure out. Can you pick Dree up and take her to Sommer? Mom's boyfriend said he rented a hotel for the weekend and I don't want to mess that up."

"I got it. And Dreek." I turned around.

"Yea."

"Don't kill her. She just told you she was pregnant and whether you love her or not, she's carrying your baby too."

22

"I'll try not to." I stormed out and drove to the house Queenie and I used to stay at. Right now, I needed time to myself to figure shit out. I hope Queenie doesn't come tonight because I can't guarantee she'll make it through the night.

Jiao

"Tell me what happened right now before I kill you." I couldn't see the person and the voice was unrecognizable.

"Kill me then. I'm over all of this. I miss my mom and I'm ready to be with her."

"Your wish is my command."

Lord forgive me for my sins. I closed my eyes and prepared myself for the fate I was about to receive.

"Put that gun away asshole. You know if she were awake, she'd kick your ass." I heard Sommer yelling.

"I am awake and I'm going to beat his ass later." I looked at Jaime who had a big ass grin on his face.

"You stay talking shit. No wonder you and Dreek get along so well." I started crying for no reason.

"What's wrong sis?" Sommer ran to me and took my hand in hers.

"I'm going to miss him so much. He's going to miss the baby being born."

"Jiao, it has to be this way. I know you love him but if he finds you." I nodded.

"I know." I sat up the best I could and noticed a bandage on my leg and one on the top of my shoulder.

"He really tried to kill me." Neither of them said a word.

"What happened Jiao?" Sommer asked. She never made it to the party. I explained everything that went down and she was shocked.

"Bitch, you never told me you shot his brother. I remember hearing about it and how Dreek went crazy looking for the killer. I mean he was on a fucking rampage my dad said."

"Sommer, he killed my mom and it was only right."

"Jiao, I don't fault you at all for avenging your mom's death. If Dreek can't understand why you did it, then it's his problem."

"How did I get here?"

"Oh, that's where I come in." Jaime said grinning.

I remember him knocking on my window and telling me to get in the car with him. He carried me inside and I blacked out. I woke up and heard someone say they were taking my life and told them to go ahead. I never paid any mind that it was his crazy ass.

Jaime and I became really close too once I got with Dreek. Him and Robert were the only two friends of Dreek's I spoke too. He would tell me how much Dreek loved me and he needed time to understand what he was going through. His mom and everyone else wanted us together but he couldn't or wouldn't give in to what he was feeling and tell me. It took me mentioning the pregnancy and almost walking away for him to admit he loved me. Unfortunately, other shit unfolded and all hell broke loose.

Now here I am at Sommer's parents pool house. Sommer told me Percy sent a message and told her to come get me, but she never made it in time, which is why Jaime saved me. He called her and she told him where to take me. The two of them were lifesavers and I planned on making sure I thanked them.

"Fuck! Percy is at the door." We all looked at the camera and he had Dree with him. Her parents had cameras all through the house.

"He can't see me Sommer. He's going to tell Dreek. Oh my God, I have to get out of here."

"Jiao, he's not going to find you." Jaime said trying to calm me down.

"Wait here. Don't come out." I nodded and we watched her open the door on camera. He said a few words and she must've been playing the role of hearing what happened because she covered her mouth and appeared to be upset. A few minutes later, she closed the door but had Dree with her. I assumed she would take her upstairs.

"JIAO." She screamed out and came running to me. I gave her a hug without letting her know how much pain I was in.

"Why did you leave? Daddy is looking for you? Are you coming over?" She bombarded me with questions.

"Dree, before I answer any questions, I need you to promise me that you won't tell daddy you saw me. You think you can do that for me?"

"Why? He misses you Jiao."

"He told you that?"

"No, but when he looked at all the pictures in your phone, he couldn't stop smiling." I smiled.

"Dree, come sit." I moved over to the couch.

"I did some things a few years ago."

"To uncle Bash, right?"

"How'd you know?"

"Queenie said you caused all the problems at my nana's party and its because you hurt uncle Bash. What did you do?" I hated Queenie for opening her mouth.

"Honey, what I did was wrong and I only did it because he did something to hurt me."

"Daddy said you're not supposed to do tit for tat, unless someone hits you." I grinned. He is a piece of work. He is tit for tat all day with his spiteful ass.

"It's true and I shouldn't have done it. However, I'm sorry and I want daddy to forgive me but he probably won't."

"But he will Jiao. Please come back."

"Dree, I promise to stay in touch with you, wherever I go."

"But how? Daddy has your phone and.-"

"I know your phone number by heart Dree. I will call you every night and you can call me but only if you don't tell daddy."

"I don't know Jiao. It's a big secret and he's going to be mad at me."

"How about this? You don't say anything to daddy and I promise to visit you here too." I hated to make her deceive Dreek but I wanted her to know I wasn't leaving. She lost her mom and to lose me too, would probably devastate her.

"Ok, but when the other lady has the baby, I won't be able to come as much. I'm going to be a big sister and the baby will need me." That's when it hit me. I forgot about Queenie mentioning a pregnancy and Dreek being mad. How he could though when it's his fault? He knew the consequences of sleeping with her unprotected.

"I understand. Let's get you ready for bed." I told her and she refused to go in Sommer's parents' house. She went in the bedroom and laid down.

"What are you going to do?" Sommer asked. Jaime left when Dree came because he didn't want her to see him and tell her dad. She would put two and two together and we didn't want that.

"I don't know. Do you have any burner phones here?"

"Why?"

"I just need to hear his voice Sommer."

"J."

"Please. I need this." She sucked her teeth and walked in the big house. She came out with a regular house phone and handed it to me.

"He's going to trace this phone."

"The number won't show up because it's my dad's old phone when he was the connect."

"Are you sure?"

"Positive." I dialed his number and blew my breath out. The phone rang a few times and when he answered, my heart melted.

"I'm sorry Dreek."

"Jiao. Where the fuck are you?"

"Dreek, go to my house and get the letter I left for you on the table."

"I already did. Where are you?" *Damn, did he go there to kill me?*

"I'm gone and don't try to find me."

"Jiao, did you lose my son?" I started crying in the phone.

"FUCKKKKKKK!" He yelled and I hung up. I couldn't lie and tell him I did when I knew one day, I'd see him.

"Where are you going?" I started putting clothes on.

32

"I need to see him Sommer. He thinks I lost the baby and.-"

"Not right now Jiao. He's upset after hearing what you did to his brother and losing the baby."

"But I didn't lose it. Maybe if he sees' me he'll forgive me and we can move past it. I can't leave him Sommer. I just can't. He's my everything." I broke down crying.

"Give him some time to calm down, then at least call to talk and see where his head is at. But right now, emotions are high with both of you and seeing him may really cause you to lose the baby. I know it hurts sis but its what's best right now." I continued crying until I fell asleep.

Queenie

When I walked in the party and saw Dreek kissing the Chinese bitch, I knew I'd lost him for good. He never showed public affection and he hated kissing, or so he said. Then to hear him confess his love for her, broke my heart in two. How dare he fall for a woman he's only known a short time but couldn't even say he missed me? It was time for me to push my plan to terminate her ass, up.

Lucky for me, I didn't need to because Dreek lost it when he found out she's the one who almost killed Bash. She screamed how she wanted to blow his brains out and I thought Dreek was going to kill her with his bare hands but the guys held him back. He was like the fucking incredible hulk.

I was shocked he didn't come after me when she ran out, but he did black out over his daughter. After he cursed me out, they walked back in the party and I sat in the corner watching him go through her phone. I know it was hers because there was a pink case on it. He had a smile on his face and it made me angrier. Here he was about to kill her and now he's smiling at shit. I walked out the side door and bounced to my friends' house.

"What are you doing here?" He opened the door and stepped to the side.

"I wanted to see you." He sucked his teeth and sat on the couch. He picked the remote to his video game up and started playing.

"Stop acting like you don't want me here." I stood in front of the television and began stripping. He leaned back watching me and stroking his dick.

"Damn, you sexy."

"So are you." I sat on his lap and kissed him. I loved the way he made love to my mouth with his tongue. My body was on fire and he knew it. His fingers were working my insides and his thumb worked my clit.

"Sssssss baby. Damn it feels good."

"How good." He sucked on my neck and then my breasts.

"Real good. Shitttttt." I moaned out and let him make love to me. Dreek only fucked me and has since the day we've started sleeping together. But Marcus, he made sure to cater to every part of my body.

Marcus is one of Dreek's soldiers and has been working under him for about five years. He isn't close with Dreek like Jaime and Robert but he is definitely a person who brings in a lot of money for him. The only problem is, he's not a boss and the way my life is set up, I need to make sure if I ever leave Dreek, the person can finance my lifestyle. Yes, he gives me money but it's not as long as Dreek's.

If Dreek ever found out about Marcus, he'd probably kill both of us. He's never put a title on us but everyone in his camp knew I was off limits. However, the liquor caught up to us one night and we spent the night together.

In the beginning, Marcus wanted to tell Dreek and face his consequences but after some persuading and promises to give him this good pussy he loves, he changed his mind. That was two months ago and we've been at it ever since.

It's been quite a few times where he's asked me to leave Dreek but I couldn't do it. I refused to allow any woman access to Dreek but somehow the Chinese bitch snuck in and got him to fall in love. I even tried to poison his brain about her and Robert sleeping together. It didn't work as you can see. I had plans for her though and I'm going to make sure they happen when she shows her face again.

"Stay the night." Marcus said kissing on my neck as I clasped my bra together.

"You know I can't."

"Queenie, I'm over this bullshit. You claim you're not really together but you're always running home to him. If you don't figure shit out, I'm moving on." He had his arm over his forehead staring at the ceiling.

"Aww baby. I miss you too at night. Look. He's going away again Friday. We can stay together all week." He smiled and pulled me down on him.

"I'm game. You still need to figure what you want. I ain't no side nigga and it's plenty of bitches out here."

"I wish you would." He laughed.

"How you threatening me and you have a man?"

"Because we all know Dreek is for everyone. You however, are all mine."

"Yea ok. Get out of here before I make you strip again." I had to smirk. If it weren't late, I'd definitely go another round.

"I love you babe." I said.

"I love you too." He kissed me and closed the door. I had a smile on my face the entire way to the car until I saw some bitch named Mandy who couldn't stand me, riding by. I heard the brakes on her car screech as she stopped in front of me.

"Hmmm. I wonder if Dreek knows about this." She had a sneaky grin on her face.

"What you want Mandy and Marcus was giving me money for Dreek."

"Yea, ok." I reached in my purse and took out a knot full of money. It was from Dreek yesterday when he gave it to me to go shopping. She didn't know that.

"Say what you want, but your shirt being inside out and your hair all over our head says different." I looked down and sucked my teeth. How did I not know?

"If you say one word."

"I won't say shit if you let me fuck him."

"WHAT?"

"I heard Dreek has a lot to offer and I want some."

39

"You're crazy as hell, if you think.-"

"I don't think. I know. The next time you see me at the club speaking with him, don't get in your feelings. He's your man and I'll be the side chick alright." She winked and pulled off. I guess it won't be so bad if he fucks her. She won't be in his life long because Dreek fucks them and leaves. I've been around for all the other bitches; one more won't be too bad.

I pulled up to Dreek's house after I left Marcus, to see if he was there. At least if he were home, it would give me piece of mind that he wasn't with her. I waited for a while and he came out, hopped in his car and took off. I tried to follow but he dipped in and out of lanes so fast, I couldn't keep up. Yup, I was still watching him even after I fucked someone else.

Once I parked in front of my condo, I hit the alarm on my car, locked the door, started the shower to get in and thought about what transpired tonight. Jiao is going to get what's coming to her and I can't fucking wait. In the meantime, at least I came enough tonight with my side nigga to put me straight to sleep.

Sommer

"Oh my Gawddddd it hurts so bad." I screamed out and squeezed Percy's hand.

"You have to push babe. Come on. She's almost here." I rolled my eyes. Not for telling me to push but for calling me babe.

I hadn't spoken to Percy since the baby shower. I mean we have talked when he dropped the kids off but it was strictly about them and nothing else. He's sent flowers, cards and a bunch of other shit, but I could care less about all of it. He showed me his true colors and I'm not sure if I could ever forgive him.

"Here comes the head." The doctor said. I hated when they did that. Half the time they couldn't see shit but amped you up to keep pushing, knowing it hurt.

"Oh shit Sommer."

"What? What's wrong?"

"Nothing. Her head popped out." He dropped my hand, went to the bottom of the bed and started recording. I swear he gets on my nerves.

"One more push Sommer." Percy said and looked at me with a huge smile on his face. I put my chin in my chest and pushed as hard as I could. I felt something gush out and a huge release. My daughter screamed and all I could do was lay there and try to catch my breath.

"You did good Sommer." He wiped my face with a towel and kissed my forehead.

"What's her name mommy?" The nurse asked placing her on my chest.

"Raven Susie Miller."

"That's a pretty name." Percy took her from me and sat down on the chair staring at her. Even though she was just born, you saw him. He sat there until it was time to take her to the nursery.

"Can we come in yet?" I heard my mom ask.

The doctor had finished stitching me up and the nurse gave me a sponge bath. Housekeeping was changing my sheets and Percy went behind the nurse to stay close to Raven. I didn't bother him about it because too many people be snatching babies from nurseries.

"Hey mommy. Daddy." They each gave me a hug and kiss.

"I can't wait to see my grand baby." Susie said smiling extra hard.

"She's not your grand baby." I heard and all of us turned around. I had no idea who this woman was but by the looks on my father's face, he did.

"Charlotte what are you doing here?"

"Charlotte?" I knew the name but never saw her face.

I sent a text to Percy and told him to get here quick. I looked at the woman who appeared to be disheveled and high. Her hair was in a short ponytail that barely fit in the rubber band. Her face as sunken in but you could still tell she used to be pretty.

44

"Yes Charlotte." She started walking closer and Susie stood in front of me. I tried to stand but I was in a lot of pain and Percy must've noticed because he came running to me.

"What's wrong babe?" This time I didn't get mad.

"I don't think she wants to see her mother Percy." I instantly began to shake. Percy pulled me on his lap as I shook and held me tight. When I finished he handed me a cup of water and asked what the fuck was going on.

"This piece of shit woman thinks that after twenty-five years she can come in here and see my daughter and grandbaby." I saw Susie taking her earrings off.

"Whoa. What you mean daughter. I ain't know you had kids." Now I was confused as to how he knew Charlotte.

"Yup. I have one daughter and this is her."

"You don't even know her name. That's sad." My father said trying to keep Susie calm.

"You're shitting me right?" Percy was having a hard time believing it.

"How do you know her Percy." He blew his breath.

"Mannnn, we been serving her for years. Had I known who she was, no one would have given her anything and from here on out she won't get shit. How did you know she was here?"

"Some bitch came on the street looking for her baby daddy Percy. One of your workers told her you were with your woman giving birth. I didn't pay the shit any mind until one of the guys asked if you were still with the old connects daughter and we all know who the old connect is." She gave my dad a fake smile. Susie didn't like that and smacked the shit out of her.

"You hit like a bitch." Charlotte wiped the blood off her lip and kept talking.

"Damn Percy had I known you were with my daughter, I would have let you sample her momma's pussy." I moved them out the way and started beating the shit out of her. I don't know why it made me upset that she offered Percy pussy when we weren't together, but it did. I felt him lift me off her.

"Sommer, you're going to bust your stitches baby." Susie said and came to sit next to me on the bed.

"That's a real pretty name. Who named you?" Charlotte was getting up off the ground. One of her eyes were closed and her nose was bleeding.

"I did." Susie said proudly.

"You gotta go. My girl don't want you here." I saw my dad staring at Charlotte with nothing but hatred in his eyes.

"Fine. I'm going."

"Don't come back." I shouted.

47

"Oh, but this piece of shit can be around?" She pointed to my dad.

"He's been for twenty-five years. Where have you been?"

"Oh, I've been around, ain't that right love?" She grabbed my dad's crotch and I gagged. He twisted her wrist and almost broke it.

"What's that supposed to mean?" Susie stood up.

"Just that big daddy here, missed this good pussy and on many occasions called me up to fuck. Remember two years ago when we stayed in the hotel all weekend sexing each other down?" I wanted to throw up in my mouth.

"You gotta go. You causing problems with your bullshit lies." Percy started pushing her out the door.

"I may be on drugs but there are two things you should know about me. One… I will never lie on my pussy. If I fucked you, I'll say it and two… know that I had two abortions by him. And before you ask, don't judge my appearance because my pussy is A1 and always will be. Good-bye. I'll see you soon love." She blew a kiss to my dad and walked out. I looked over at Susie and she had tears streaming down her face.

Susie couldn't have kids because of endometriosis and always wanted to adopt but my dad said no. If they didn't have children naturally, he didn't want them. He never wanted them growing up looking for their real parents and leaving them heartbroken. I believed it to be the reason but I'm not so sure now. Susie was the perfect woman for him and he cheated with a fucking crack head. A crack head who left her addicted baby in the hospital.

"Susie." My dad reached for her and she moved away as if he had the plague.

"I'm moving out."

"No you're not." She stopped and turned around and smacked the shit out of him. My dad didn't even attempt to retaliate. I don't think Percy would let him anyway but you never know.

"How dare you try and tell me I can't leave? You've been sticking your dick in a fucking whore, crack head, piece of shit woman for years. I've been nothing but good to you. I begged you to adopt a kid or even do surrogacy and you shot me down each time. Yet, you slept with her and almost gave her two more babies. Babies you know I couldn't naturally have. I was your ride or die chic when the bitch left my daughter in the hospital. I took care and adopted her. You are a fucking bastard and I hate you. If you even think about trying to stop me from leaving, I'll cut your dick off and you know I'll do it."

My father stood there speechless and Percy stood there staring at me. I had tears coming down my face because I know what it feels like to be cheated on. Kevin did it to me and I thought Percy did. Susie loved my father unconditionally and he backslid with the same woman who didn't care enough for me to stop getting high. How could he be ok laying down with her?

"Sommer, I'm sorry you had to witness this. You are still my daughter and I will call you when I'm settled." She kissed my forehead.

"I want to see my grandbaby the same day she comes home." I hugged her and promised to bring her by. When she left I stared at my dad with disgust.

"Sommer."

"Don't dad. I understand men cheat but why did it have to be with her? I was addicted to crack daddy. CRACK. I live with the shakes because of her actions and you've been sleeping with her all this time. She left me in the hospital and never looked back. Susie was there like she's always been. How could you do that to her, to me?"

"I don't know Sommer. I went to her a few times to see if she wanted to get to know you and each time she turned the choice down. She knew a lot about my operation because before Susie, she was there and did a lot of illegal shit for me. Charlotte had and still has a disk of some sort she won't give me that holds deadly information on it. I'm talking about things that could even send him to jail." He pointed to Percy who held his head down.

"Why didn't you get it instead of sleeping with her?"

"Ohhhh. If it were as easy with her as you think."

"What you mean?"

"Sommer, I think what your father is trying to say is, if anything happens to her, the disk will get into the wrong hands. It's her security to stay alive."

"It doesn't explain why you slept with her."

"You think I wanted to cheat on Susie?" I raised my eyebrow.

"I love the hell out of Susie. She is the only woman I ever loved and its hurting me that she's going to leave me over this. I had no choice if we wanted to be happy. Charlotte knew exactly what she was doing when she came here. She knows who you are from all the photos she's seen on my phone. There's a reason she came here today and it ain't for a happy reunion, I can tell you that."

"I'm going to find out." Percy said standing up and walking my dad outside. What in the hell is going on?

Percy

"Sommer, I had no idea she was your mom." He shut the door and came to sit by me.

"Its ok Percy."

"It's not though. Had I known, she never would have been able to buy from me. It may be a little over a year since we've known one another but it could've been a year for her to be clean."

"I don't believe she wants to be clean. If she's blackmailing my dad as he says, she must have a reason but what is it? Who is she working for?" As she said those words, Hector stuck out for some reason. Did he have a crackhead working for him? He couldn't, because her dad has been out the game for some years now but then again if the information could hurt us, then he may have her doing his dirty work. I had to hit Dreek up.

"CODE ADAM!" We heard on the intercom of the hospital.

"OH MY GOD PERCY. GO GET RAVEN. GO PLEASE." I had no idea why she screamed but I ran out the room and into the nursery.

"Sir, you can't be in here." I paid the nurses no mind as they all stood there panicking with security. I searched the room for my daughter and once I laid eyes on her, I snatched her up and took her in the room with Sommer. A nurse followed with the crib thing they lay the babies in and shut the door behind us.

"Thank God you have her." Sommer checked the bracelet to make sure she was the right baby.

"What's going on Sommer? Why did you scream like that?" She wiped her tears and kissed my daughter.

"Code Adam means a child is missing. I was scared it was Raven." I turned to the nurse.

"Is that true?" The nurse nodded.

"Someone came in the nursery asking for a baby with the last name Miller. We checked all the babies and none of them had the last name." Sommer covered her mouth and I became angrier.

"When we told her there was no one by that name. She pulled a gun out and threatened to kill us all. I pressed the button for a Code Adam, knowing security would contact the cops and come running up. She started panicking and ran out the room and we're not at liberty to make an attempt to stop her."

"Where is she?"

"We don't know. Your wife had every right to have you come and get your daughter." I smiled when she called Sommer my wife.

"I'm going to need to see the video."

"You can talk to the head of security. He's on his way up with the cops." I told her to tell him I'd like to speak with him. Who the hell is here trying to take my daughter?

"You think it was your mom?" I asked and she shrugged her shoulders.

"Percy, I don't want to stay here any longer." I had her move over and laid in the bed.

"You have to stay at least til morning but I promise not to leave this room without you." She put her head on my shoulder and I placed my daughter on my chest. Shit, was getting crazy and we had to get it under control before it's too late.

****

"Percy, can you keep an eye on Raven? I'm going to visit my dad. I want to know more about Charlotte."

"Yup." I kissed her cheek and went to check on my daughter. It's been two weeks since we left the hospital and she had me staying at her house with her. During the day, I'd be out handling business but the minute it turned dark, she was calling to see where I was.

Lately, she's been over her dad's house a lot. I know she keeps saying it has something to do with finding out as much as she can about Charlotte but something is off. I'm going to let it be for now but if I find out she on some other shit, I'll fucking kill her.

"What up?" Dreek said coming in the house. He was stressed the hell out over Jiao losing his son and Queenie wasn't making his life any easier. Every time he was out she needed this or that for the baby. My boy hasn't even been to the barbershop and he owns it.

"Nothing. Sommer left so I have Raven and Percy Jr. I see your master let you out the house." I started laughing but he wasn't.

"I'm ready to fucking kill Queenie."

"Damn, it's that bad?"

"You don't even know the half. Dree is always with my mom now that Sommer had the baby. I only get to see her if I go there because she refuses to be around Queenie. I can't help but wonder where J is and if she's ok? Then, my brother keeps trying to talk to me but I can't be bothered right now."

"Bash, didn't know she was your girl Dreek. You can't be mad he blasted that Jiao was the one who tried to kill him. I'm not saying it would have gone differently but you should definitely find out if he did kill her mom."

"That's the thing Percy. I don't want to know because then it gives me reason to forgive her and I can't."

"Are you serious Dreek? Jiao, is your soul mate, the only woman who has ever got your mean ass to say I love you.

Yea, she may have made a mistake and I get you're mad. However, are you ready to give up on what the two of you could've had and still can?"

"It doesn't matter. I can't find her and she's probably scared to even be anywhere near me."

"I wouldn't be around you either. Your entire body started blowing up when you heard her say it."

"Fuck you." He stood up and took Raven from me.

"Damn man. I remember when Dree and Percy Jr. were this small. I can't believe she lost my son and I don't know what the bitch at the house is having."

"I've been meaning to ask; how did you end up sliding in her raw." When he told me the story I had to laugh.

"What?"

"Queenie drugged your ass and if you don't know it, I suggest you take the cup you still have in your car and get it tested." His entire facial expression changed.

"Nah, she ain't crazy. You think so."

"Dreek, you have never been too intoxicated where you don't remember what you did the next day. How many times have you drank an entire bottle of Henney and still been fine the following day? Or you could be drunk as a skunk and still strap up? Bro, I hate to tell you but she did. Plus, she was too anxious to shout it out in front of Jiao." I saw him thinking about what I said.

"I hope she ain't do any stupid shit like that."

"Go get it tested bro and be ready for the results." He handed me Raven and went straight out the door. Queenie is a sneaky bitch and I guarantee its exactly what's he did. There's no way my boy is stupid enough to run up in her raw after all these years. I just don't see it.

Two hours later Sommer came strolling in with the scent of a guy lingering on her clothes. We're not a couple but its mad disrespectful to come in the house smelling of a dude. Let me come in smelling like a woman, she'd be ready to shoot me. I handed her Raven and grabbed my keys to leave.

"Hey, where you going?" She came behind me and grabbed my hand.

"Why?"

"I don't know. I miss you and us. I thought we could talk when you get back. I have some things I need to get off my chest."

"You mean about the dude you've been seeing." Her eyes grew wide.

"Percy, it's not what you think."

"So, you have been around a guy."

"Yes, but not in the way you think. He's helping me out with something."

"What?" I folded my arms and stared at her.

"I can't tell you." I turned to leave.

"Percy, I know we're not together but I would never sleep with another man, let alone kiss one. I'm in love with you but I need you to trust me. Trust enough to know I would never allow you to walk around looking like a fool, knowing I'm with someone else. It's not me and never will be."

"Is it Kevin?"

"HELL NO!" She yelled out and scared my daughter.

"I have been extra careful not to run into him. Percy, I love you." She pulled me in for a kiss.

"I swear Sommer if I find out you're fucking around."

"I wouldn't do that to you."

"Go feed my daughter." I told her when Raven started getting cranky. She walked away with a sad face. I wanted to stay but I needed to get over to the warehouse. Some shit kicked off and I didn't want any of it finding my doorstep.

Dreek

"Hey sexy." I heard and looked up from my seat in VIP.

It was this chick named Mandy who had been dying for my attention for a few years now but Queenie always interfered.

The club wasn't too crowded but enough for security to be tight. I told him to allow her in and I had to lick my lips. Mandy is one sexy ass bitch, if I say so myself.

She had a caramel skin complexion with an average body but a firm ass. She wore a long straight weave like most women these days and her dress barely covered her body. Her makeup was beat as chicks say and the earring on the top of her lip was sexy too. There wasn't anything wrong with her as of right now.

"What up Mandy?" She sat next to me and started rubbing on my leg. I had to laugh because she was straight to the point. It's no secret she wanted to fuck but shorty didn't even have a drink yet and she's acting thirsty.

"I see you waste no time."

"Not when I've been waiting years for you." She whispered in my ear and stuck her tongue in it.

"Oh yea." I looked down on the dance floor and had to blink my eyes a few times to make sure I wasn't bugging. It's been two months since I've seen or heard from Jiao so to see her in here made me jump up.

"Where you going?" Mandy pushed me down on the couch and sat on top of me. Her dressed was now over her ass and revealing that she wore no panties. She leaned in to kiss me and I turned my head. Jiao is the only woman who has ever tasted my lips and it will stay like that.

"Oh, you're one of those. It's cool. We don't have to kiss because I'm sure you'll please me in other ways." She stood up and stripped out of her dress making everyone in VIP stare at her.

"Yo, put your clothes on."

"What, you don't want anyone to see what's yours?"

"Frankly, I don't give a fuck about you showing your pussy. I do care about the feds coming up in here thinking I'm running a brothel or some shit."

"My bad."

"I get you wanna fuck me but you're going to need to come stronger than this. I get pussy thrown at me all the time. If you want me to fuck you, find a reason to make me." I stood up and pushed her out my way.

Mandy definitely had me ready to fuck but she was being too extra. I don't need this shit getting back to Queenie and she gets n my nerves more than she already is.

"Yo, I thought Jiao was missing." Robert said and came walking behind me.

"Where she go?"

"She was right here? Yo, what happened to the blasian chick sitting here?" The new bartender shrugged his shoulders.

She couldn't have gone far but with Mandy on my lap for those few minutes, who knows. Robert and I went outside to check and the only people standing there was security.

"It was her right?" I asked Robert to confirm he saw the same person.

"It sure as hell looked like her. Go look on the cameras." We both went in the office and before I could pull the cameras up, I heard some commotion outside the door.

"Really Mandy." She had a bottle of something and a brand-new pack of condoms.

"You said make you want to fuck me. I figure a little more liquor and protection is enough, don't you think." Robert smirked at me.

"Get your stupid ass over here." She sashayed in my direction.

"I'm out yo. Be careful because she's known for trying to trap a nigga." Robert whispered and nodded his head at Mandy. One would think we had beef after I whooped his ass over Jiao but it was all love. He apologized and told me he understood. It's crazy how men can move on from bullshit but chicks hold on forever.

"This is a nice office. I can't wait to fuck you looking down on the crowd."

"Never gonna happen. Let's roll." She sucked her teeth.

I opened the door and led her out the back door. There's an area out here where some of us come smoke to relax and do exactly what I'm about to do now. We walked over to the chair that had cushions on it and sat down. I took the blunt from the side of my ear, lit it and watched her take off the clothes, I made her put on a little while ago.

"Suck my dick and if you mess up one time, I'm out."

"Well damn."

"You want this dick or not?" I grabbed her wrist and forced her down on the ground. She wrapped her lips around it and I laid my head back staring in the sky smoking. Mandy was doing a good job but I wanted to fuck.

"Get up."

"You didn't like it?"

"I just wanna fuck. Don't ask no question." I took the condom out my pocket and rolled it down on my dick. I'll be damned if I use the one she had and it has holes in it. I trust no one.

"Ahhh fuck Dreek." She yelled when I pushed in.

Her pussy was tight as hell and gushy but the fact she kept complaining started pissing me off. I tried to change positions to make it easier on her. I took my man out, tossed the condom in the trash on the side of the chair and pulled my jeans and boxers up.

"Why you stop?"

"Do me a favor and come find me when you can take dick."

"Nigga I can." She was mad.

"Not this dick. You pushed me out with your pussy every time."

"I have to get used to you."

"If you say so."

"Dreek let me try again."

"I'm good yo." I walked back to the door and waited. I wasn't leaving her out here.

"Thank you." She said as I held the door. I grabbed her hand.

"Don't be embarrassed. Some women can take it and others can't. It doesn't mean the pussy ain't good because it was decent." I saw her grin.

"Like you said, maybe you have to get used to it." She kissed my cheek and told me she's buying a dildo big as my dick so she could. The next time she'll be ready. I laughed. The shit women do for a man's attention is crazy.

"I love the way you feel Dreek. Shittttt baby." Mandy yelled out.

It's been a few weeks since our first encounter and we've fucked quite a bit. She called me up two days after the first time and begged me to give her another chance. I did and she still had problems adjusting to it but being in her almost every day, made her comfortable. She was handling me like a pro now.

"Keep riding it. I'm about to cum." I smacked her ass and lifted her off when I felt my nut coming up. She snatched the condom off like she always does and enjoyed swallowing. My phone went off as she kissed her way up my stomach. I picked it up and noticed the text was from an unknown number. I opened it up.

Unknown: There's not a day that goes by where you're not on my mind. I miss you so much Dreek. When you told me you loved me, all I wanted to do was jump in your arms and let you take me home to make love to me. I know you're angry

with me for what I did to Bash, who I had no idea was your

brother but I had to for my mom.

I want to hear your voice so bad, I want to hear you

yelling at me or something but its better this way. We can't be

together and I know you've moved on but know I love you with

all my heart.

She sent a bunch of red hearts after the text. I can't lie it

definitely had me in my feelings. Jiao still had an effect on me,

regardless if she was present or not.

I wanted to call back but the number was unknown,

which is crazy because I didn't even know a message could be

sent like that. I put my phone on the bed, stood up and began to

get dressed. It's about time for me to speak to my brother about

what went down.

Ever since my mom's party I had been avoiding him

like the plague. I felt he knew about Jiao and never told me.

I'm not saying it would change my feelings for her but I wouldn't have been with her at all.

I threw my shirt over my head and grabbed my things. Mandy gave me a crazy look as she laid there naked. We usually had sex a few times a day but not this time. I had some shit to figure out.

"Are you coming back?"

"I'm not sure but the room is paid up for a week so feel free to stay the entire time."

"If you're not coming back, I'll just go home." Here she was acting like a brat.

"I may or may not return. You can take your chances if you want. I have your number if by some chance I do come and you're not here. Just make sure no one touches this pussy besides me." I hit her with the peace sign and left.

I know some may ask why I told her not to fuck anyone else. It has absolutely nothing to do with me caring about her or anything of the sort. I just don't want another nigga running up in her and when it's my turn she can't take it again, like in the beginning.

Again, Jiao is the only woman to this day; I will kill for if she was with someone else.

I made it to my moms' house and saw my brothers' car there. I guess there's no time like the present.

Bash

I was sitting in my moms' kitchen listening to my niece Dree talk to me about a baby my brother was having. At first, I assumed she was speaking of the Queenie chick who announced her pregnancy at the same time Jiao mentioned losing hers.

Each time she spoke and said something about him, she'd look at my mom and change up real quick. I'm no fool and I know when something is going on. I was about to address it when the door opened and Dree went running to Dreek.

He had been avoiding me at all cost since the party and today we were about to deal with the shit. I feel bad he fell for the woman who almost killed me but why take it out on me? I admit when he didn't kill her, I knew right then and there, his feelings were involved. Anyone else, Dreek would've murdered without asking questions or giving them time to explain. He was sick when Jiao said she lost the baby. My mom said he wouldn't come out the house for the first few days. She had to go over there and break him out of the funk.

As I'm sure everyone knows, Dreek is not an easy person to get along with. I'm not sure how the chick got him to love her but my mom adored her. She said Jiao made him respect her and fall in love, which no woman in all of his twenty-nine years has been able to do. I give her a lot of credit because any woman would have walked away. I wish I would have walked away from Candiance because then she wouldn't be dead.

"I'm here and I want to know what happened." He asked Dree to go in the other room while we spoke. My mom sat down too and listened.

"Candiance was the woman I met and told you about."

"I remember and when Jiao showed me the photo of her, I knew it was a reason she looked familiar." I never brought Candiance around but he was the only one who knew anything about her.

"She was beautiful, with a great spirit and heart. She was older than me by ten years but fuck it; age ain't nothing but a number, especially to men.

I ran into her one day at the Chinese restaurant her husband owned and immediately began flirting with her. I mean, she was drop dead gorgeous and you couldn't tell her age by looking at her. Anyway, I went there a lot and on one occasion she was crying. I asked her if she were ok and it's how we ended up being together.

Candiance was married to a man who gave her everything but still cheated. She didn't know how many times at first but once was enough for her. She found the text messages; receipts to hotels and large amounts of money began disappearing from their account. Whenever she asked, he'd say it was for the business. Needless to say, she found out one of the women was someone they both were friends with and confronted her. She beat her up twice from what I hear."

"I know that's right. Bitches ain't shit." My mom said shaking her head.

"We started meeting up at my house; hotels and I even took her on a few vacations across the world. She would tell her husband it was for peace of mind and he'd allow it because he tried to make up for the cheating. The entire year and a half we were together, not once did anyone know. Both of us had already admitted to being in love and I gave up all my ho's once she informed me that they were no longer living together. I didn't believe her until she invited me over.

Her daughter had no idea because she was off doing her own thing. She had a small apartment and they made sure to stay at the house together whenever she came over. I think her daughter knew but refused to believe her parents were unhappy. I never knew Jiao was her daughter until I made it to Candiance in the hotel room.

I had just left you Dreek when she called and said she was ready for me. I loved how she catered to me and made sure to make each sexual encounter somewhat different from the last time and a nigga couldn't wait to get to her.

I parked in the back and took the elevator up. I noticed the door was cracked, pulled my gun out and checked the room. She was on the ground with blood coming out her mouth. I reminisced on the night she was murdered.

"Bash, go."

"Hell no. I have to get you some help."

"Please Bash. My daughter is on her way and I don't want her to see you. I want her memory of me to be perfect."

"Candiance."

"Bash, I love you baby. I'll see you at the hospital ok." *I felt the tears trickling down my face. The woman I was in love with was dying in front of me. I knew she wouldn't make it if I didn't get her help.*

"I love you too. Candiance, make sure you fight to live ok. I'm going to sit outside the hospital now. When you're better, I'm taking you away from here. We're moving away." I wiped her tears and stood up

"Go." She said and I walked out the room. I saw a chick staring at me and going in the same direction as I ran past. I heard a loud scream as the elevator stopped on the floor. I stepped on and I felt Candiance leaving this earth. I can't say how but you know when your soul mate is no longer around. I got to my car and broke down. I watched the cops, ambulance and coroner pull up. I knew for sure then she was gone. *My mom looked like she was about to cry listening to me.*

"It took me a few weeks to get out of my funk and when I did, you dragged me to the bar. As I was standing out there using the bathroom, Jiao approached me and tried to kill me and at times I wish you weren't there to save me because I could be with Candiance again. When I came to at the hospital, you had me leave and stay in California until you found the person responsible.

Three years went by and you still had no idea, until the night of the party. It's hard to find someone when you're looking in the wrong place. No one thought a chick shot me and I was embarrassed, so I never mentioned it. The look on Jiao's face when she did it, let me know she thought I killed her mom. I understood and accepted my fate. However, now that I'm back, it's my duty to find out who did it and I'll stop at nothing until I do."

"Dreek, you can't kill her." I said and he looked at me.

"At mommy's party, I wanted her to die and for you to find out but after thinking back and realizing why she did it, I get it. She tried to avenge her mom's death as would we, if it were ma."

"Andreek look." My mom turned to face him.

"Jiao, loves you. I mean really loves you. I mean she has to if she stayed around for the beatings, disrespect and back and forth with Queenie. I know you love her too so why are you fighting it?"

"Ma, I don't know where she is and she lost my son."

"Baby, you haven't even attempted to look for her because if you did, you'd know exactly where she is." We both stared at my mom.

"She's not at her fathers or her apartment. Sommer has been with her parents the entire time and now she's with Percy. There's nowhere else I could think of."

"I know where she is." Dree said walking in the kitchen with her nosy self.

"How do you know?"

"Nana and I.-"

"Girl hush your mouth. Coming in here making up stories about Jiao. You know your dad don't like when you tell lies." Dreek looked at her and my niece stepped out the kitchen.

"Ma, you know where she is?" She stood up and walked out. He followed and continued asking questions.

"Dreek, even if I did, I wouldn't tell you."

"Why? Aren't you even the tad bit upset she almost killed your son? You act like you don't care." Dreek was getting angry. My mom smacked the hell out of him.

"Don't you ever come in here and ask me no stupid shit like that. Of course, I care that my son almost died. I was there from the moment he got to the hospital until the day you had him leave. I cleaned his wounds and made sure he ate well. I also made sure the doctors were taking very good care of him so don't ever question me about my son. How fucking dare you?" My mom sat on the couch with her head down.

"I'm sorry ma."

"Just go find her Dreek and don't make her suffer any longer. But know this." He turned around.

"When you see her, take it easy. She's very fragile and emotional right now and she doesn't need the stress."

"What does that mean?"

"When you find her, you'll know." He stormed out the house and sped out the driveway.

"You know where she is, don't you?"

"Yup and I ain't telling him shit. He's still dealing with the stupid Queenie bitch and probably a bunch of other ho's. She doesn't need to deal with any of that with the state she's in."

"She didn't lose the baby, did she?" My mom stood up and stretched.

"No and don't you dare tell him."

"Ma, my brother lost it when he thought she miscarried. How can you not tell him?"

"The same way you never told me she's the one who almost killed you. We asked you over and over but you never told us. She would have been dead by now and none of us would be dealing with choices of, if she should die now."

"I know ma. I'm over it though but I am going to find out who killed her mom. Whoever it is, is the reason everything is hectic. I will kill them and that's no lie." I walked out the living room and went to find Dree. I knew she wasn't lying but I also know now why my mom didn't want her to mention it.

"Dree, I thought you were supposed to keep it a secret about Jiao." She wiped her eyes.

"I am but she's having my baby brother and I know daddy would be happy if he found out. Why can't we tell him?"

"He'll find out soon enough. In the meantime, how about we go for a ride?" She hopped up and gave me a hug.

She and I spent the afternoon at the mall, then we went to the movies and on our way home, she said something that made me stop.

"That's where Jiao lives." I had to laugh.

"Are you sure?"

"Yup. I'm positive. Can we go see her?" I hesitated at first because even though I understood why she shot me, I'm not sure I wanted to be around her.

"I guess." We pulled in the parking lot and stepped out.

I noticed my brothers' car parked about ten houses down and stifled another laugh. If he only knew Jiao lived a few doors down from Queenie he would have a fit. But hey, I'm going to let him find her like my mom said.

Jiao

"I'm beating her ass after I have this baby." I spoke of the chick on Dreek's lap in the club.

"Bitch, you don't even know who she is."

"Not the point. He's not supposed to entertain bitches."

"Ugh, you fell off the face of the earth. What do you expect him to do?"

"Ugh, wait until I pop up. Shit, he's the reason we were at the club in the first place." I started crunching on the ice I had in my cup. I was six months pregnant now and my son was active as hell and greedy. I would eat a full meal and be starving a half hour later.

"You crazy as hell. Take Raven while I use the bathroom." Sommer passed me my goddaughter and left the room.

The other night I talked Sommer into going to the club with me to see Dreek. I had been depressed over not seeing him and all I wanted was to hear his voice or see his face. Surprisingly, I watched him for a good twenty minutes as he sat in VIP drinking with his boys.

I was about to make my entrance when out of nowhere some thot ass bitch walked in. The bitch had the nerve to take all of her clothes off. Once I saw that, I knew then, he had moved on and wasn't worried about me.

I cried my eyes out and made a vow to myself that I wouldn't go looking for him anymore. Low and behold, a few weeks later I sent him an emotional text message and stared at the phone for an hour waiting for a response. It wasn't until Sommer reminded me the number comes up as unknown so even if he wanted to, he couldn't. I did see he read it but how did I know Queenie didn't see and erase it? I guess I wouldn't.

"I can't wait until you have little Dreek. He's going to be a bad little thing." Sommer sat on the other side of the couch and picked her phone up. Raven was now a couple months old and nosy like her momma. She heard Sommer and tried to look all around for her.

"Don't talk about my baby. He damn sure ain't growing up like his father. Shit, no one should ever grow up like his mean ass." We both started laughing.

"That must be Jaime at the door. I asked him to bring us some pizza." Sommer said and went to answer it.

"Jiaoooooo." I heard Dree yell and saw her running towards me. How did she get here? Dreek's mom always called before she came.

"Hello Jiao." My heart stopped and I laid Raven in the bassinet Sommer had here for when she came. If he wanted to kill me, I damn sure wasn't about to allow my goddaughter to get caught in the crossfire.

"Why are you here?"

"He brought me J. I wanted to see you and my baby brother." Bash stared at my stomach and shook his head as Dree rubbed on my belly.

"My brother is going to kill you."

"Tell me something I don't know. Is it why you came?"

"Actually, my niece wanted to see you and when I say he's going to kill you, it won't be because of me but for not telling him the baby didn't die. He didn't handle it well when he thought you lost it." I plopped down on the couch and put my head in my hands.

"He asked me if I lost him and instead of answering, I started crying. I never told him no, I guess he assumed it."

"It's my fault Bash."

"How is that?"

"She tried to leave and see Dreek to let him know, but I wouldn't let her. He was angry after finding out about you and I was scared he would kill her." He nodded and agreed it could have happened.

"How is he?" I looked in his eyes and saw a little of Dreek.

"Not as good as you think. He misses you a lot Jiao."

"Did he tell you that?"

"No." I sucked my teeth.

"My brother doesn't show emotions but whenever your name comes up, all of them show on his face. Whatever you

89

did to him, made him feel things he never felt. I know you see his hardcore demeanor but I know you're the only woman who saw past it and loved him anyway." I started crying.

"I miss him so much but we can't be together. He'll never forgive me and I don't blame him."

"You haven't given him the chance Jiao. You won't tell him where you are."

"I can't risk it. He may pretend he wants to talk but what if it's a plan?" He threw his head back laughing.

"Haven't you learned anything from him? If he wants to kill you, he'll tell you, no doubt. Dreek is a nigga who don't give a fuck about your feelings and will tell you what you don't want to hear."

"You should see him Jiao. When he was talking to nana today, he looked sad when she said your name." Dree said and asked to hold Raven. Sommer walked over and helped her.

"I don't know."

"Look. I didn't think I wanted to see or talk to you either but I'm here and I get why you don't want to do it. You're scared he'll reject and give you some sort of closure you don't want. However, you won't know until call him yourself."

"Fine. Sommer give me the phone." Dree had gone in her room to watch some show on television. Yes, I had a three-bedroom condo and made sure, I had a room for her. I dialed his number in front of them and waited for him to answer.

"Hello." I heard Queenie say. I didn't speak but Sommer gestured for me to ask for him.

"Can I speak to Andreek?" I don't know why I said his full name whenever she answered.

"Well, well, well, if it isn't the almost murderer." I stared at Bash and he was shaking his head.

"Queenie can you put him on the phone?"

"He doesn't want to speak with the bitch who almost killed his brother. Matter of fact, he's been over here telling me how he's going to find, torture and then kill you for making him and his family go through that."

"I want to hear him say it." I heard him saying something in the background.

"Dreek, have you heard from the chick who almost killed Bash?"

"No, I haven't seen the bitch but trust me, I will and when I do, she better run the other way."

"Dreek, I think you should hear what she has to say."

"Fuck that bitch. Now come upstairs and sit on my dick."

"I'll be right there baby."

"Well, you heard it for yourself. He wants me to sit on his dick and we both know how good it is, so I'm out." She hung up and I threw the phone across the room. Bash and Sommer looked at me.

"How did he not know she was on the phone?"

"Knowing her, she had it where he couldn't see it. He had to be in a different room and knowing him, he wasn't paying attention."

"It doesn't change the fact of him wanting to kill me."

"Yo." Bash answered his phone.

"Ummmm. I came to visit this chick. Where you at?" Me and Sommer walked in the kitchen to give him privacy.

"Can Dree stay here?"

"Of course."

"I don't know what went down over there but he left and saw my car here. I'm out." He ran out the door and we ran to the window.

Dreek was stepping out his car and on his way up. Bash caught him and they walked to his car. I saw him looking at his phone and I thought about calling him but changed my mind. He may have not known Queenie was on the phone but he still planned on killing me. I'm good.

Dreek

I walked in the room after telling Queenie to come sit on my dick and noticed my phone wasn't up here. I went down the steps and heard her talking shit about fucking me and snapped on her when I noticed she was on my phone.

"Who were you talking to?" I snatched it out her hand before she could delete whoever it was. I'm positive she deleted Jiao's number previously.

"The Chinese girl called and.-" I yanked her up by the throat. Her feet were dangling in the air.

"I told you to stop calling her that. What did you say?" I waited for her to answer and she said nothing.

"What... did... you... say?" She pointed to my hands on her neck. I let go and she had to gasp for air.

"Dreek how could you choke me and I'm pregnant?" I ignored her and asked again.

"I told her you were going to torture and kill her. What's the big deal?"

"There's no big deal at all." I made my way up the steps and put my clothes on.

"Where are you going?" She asked waddling up the steps. She was four months pregnant with a small stomach. I stared and thought of how Jiao would have been six, had she not lost my son.

"Dreek, why are you so upset?"

I thought about what she said and I knew the reason. It was because I missed Jiao and wanted to hear her voice as much as she wanted to hear mine. I needed to make love to her and feel the way I used to when she came around. I felt lost without her and all the fucking in the world, didn't soothe me at all.

I also knew if she called, the number would be blocked and I couldn't return the call. How could I be careless and leave it around Queenie? I slammed the door and went to my car. I turned to reverse and noticed Bash's car down the parking lot. I only saw it because he has a bright yellow Charger. No one else around here had that ugly car.

"Who the chick you meet?" I asked looking in my phone when he came over to me.

"Nobody important. What's up?"

"Shit. Queenie pissed me off. I had to get out of there."

"Why you with her?"

"She's pregnant and I don't want to leave her; at least until she gives birth. Ma said stress can kill the baby and I can't lose another one."

"You believe it's your kid?"

"If you're asking if I thought Jiao's was mine? Without a doubt, I knew he was. I'm not so sure about this bitch. Something is shady as hell with her."

"Did you ask?" I raised my eyebrow.

"What bitch you know will say she's really pregnant by someone else? I'm waiting for her to have it and requesting a DNA. Momma didn't raise no fool." We stood out there talking for a few minutes before I decided to leave.

****

"Come on Dree." I yelled up the steps for her. We were going to visit her mom at the cemetery. It was her birthday and Dree wanted to see her.

We stopped at the flower store and picked some up. When we got there, it was quite a bit of people out. Some of them were older and I noticed the groundskeepers too.

"Happy Birthday mommy." Dree wiped the tombstone off and picked the roses apart. She put half a dozen on her moms and had me follow her to someone else's.

"Sommer." She looked up.

"What are you doing here?" She spoke to Dree and ignored me.

"Today's my mommy birthday. Daddy brought me here to bring flowers but I wanted to put some by Jiao's mom too."

"That's very nice and if Jiao were here, I bet she'd give you a big hug."

"Where is she Sommer?" I asked as Dree laid them down.

"Let her be Dreek. She's tired of stressing herself over you."

"I need to see her."

"For what Dreek? To torture and kill her. Queenie told us and we heard you say she needs to run the other way." I ran my hand over my head.

"Maybe you're right. I may beat the shit out of her if I see her. I mean she is the one who almost killed my brother." I don't even know why I said that. I went to walk away and turned around.

"Stay right here Dree." I moved closer.

"I forgave her for what went down with my brother when I found out what really happened. But I won't forgive her for leaving my daughter. The one who loves her and innocent in all of this."

"Dreek."

"No Sommer. She is supposed to be there for Dree." She went to speak and I stopped her.

"Don't think I don't know she calls my daughter." She looked shocked.

"So, you know she didn't leave her."

"Sommer, that's nothing when she can't take her places and spend time with her like before. My daughter loved Jiao as if she birthed her but this hiding shit is childish. I swear on everything if she doesn't show up soon, she won't ever see Dree again. Fuck with it if you want."

"DREEK! DREEK!" She yelled and cane running behind me.

"Jiao sees Dree all the time. Your daughter is the only reason she hadn't left." I stopped."

"What you mean?"

"It means she loves both of you and even though the two of you can't be together, she'll never neglect Dree."

"I don't believe you. Dree would have told me." Then I thought about the day at my mom's house when Dree said she knew where Jiao was.

"It's true Dreek. Your daughter has her own room with Jiao. And when she doesn't listen, you can bet Jiao gets in her ass. Dreek she is helping you raise her, even though you don't know. In her eyes, you're Dree's father and she's the stepmother."

"Then why won't she let me see her?"

"She's scared Dreek. Can you blame her?" I put my head down.

"We finally got her to agree to see you one day. She called and Queenie answered and said all those things to her. Jiao washed her hands with trying to meet up."

"Set it up Sommer."

"What?"

"I want to see her and until I do, Dree will be with me. It may sound crazy but it's time to face reality." I told her and walked on the drivers' side of my car.

"Dreek I don't think I can."

"Well take a picture of Dree now because it's the only way she'll see her." I put up the deuces and left her standing there. I looked in my rear-view mirror and saw her on the phone. She better make it happen or neither of them will see

Dree and I mean it.

Mandy

"I want this one Dreek." I whined a little and he smirked. He and I have been spending a lot of time together.

"Man, get whichever one you want." I pointed to the Chanel purse and told the lady to take it to the register.

We were in New York shopping and a bitch was in heaven. Lately, he's been treating me more like his girl, instead of a jump off.

In the beginning, all I wanted was dick but being around him, had me wanting more. Granted, he never spent the night, we didn't go out to eat around town and he had a pregnant chick at home but none of it mattered. His presence was appreciated whether it be an hour or two.

He never really spoke about anything though. He was very private which is a turn on. The mystery intrigues the hell out of me. I do wish we had conversations but fuck it; I'm getting what most of these chicks out here wanted, and that's his time and now him spending money on me.

"Hurry up. I'm hungry." He took a call and stepped out the store.

I grabbed the bags with my new Chanel purse, a few red bottoms and some sexy lingerie for him. He always wanted me naked when he got to the room but I figured this would enhance our sexual relations. Yea, I'm claiming Andreek Puryear and not a bitch is going to tell me otherwise.

We were out all day when we made it to the room, we couldn't keep our hands off each other.

"Dreek, I can't cum anymore." I moaned out. He had me ass up in the hotel room.

"I'm not stopping until I nut and you better not dry up." He smacked my ass and continued fucking the hell out of me. Women always say they want a man with a big dick but the shit will leave you crippled.

"I'm about to nut Mandy." I felt him pull out, turned around and sucked all of his kids out. He never came in the condom while inside me. He didn't want anymore kids right now but I will eventually get him to put one in me. At the rate we're going, I see it happening soon.

"Shit, Dreek. You always fuck me good." He ignored me, stood up and went in the bathroom to shower. He hated

104

lying in bed after sex. Once I got out the bathroom and laid down, I could hear his phone ring. I looked for him but he wasn't around so I picked it up and the caller was unknown.

"Hello." I probably shouldn't have but being he's my man, why not.

"Ummm, did I dial the wrong number? I was looking for Andreek." I knew the voice but right now it wasn't registering on who she was.

"He's here but we just finished making love to each other so he's out of it. Can I take a message?" I could tell by the way she blew her breath in the phone, I pissed her off.

"Tell him to stop making demands about seeing me and then letting you wanna be girlfriends answer his phone." I sat up on the bed.

"Hold up. You don't know me."

"I don't need to. The minute you mentioned fucking him, I already saw how petty you were. The crazy thing is, he may be fucking you but he's sending messages for me to see him. Say what you want, but you and the rest of the bitches he

105

fucks, are nothing but a distraction for the woman he really wants."

"You think he wants a woman who can't even disclose her phone number? One he has to send messages to find. Honey, if he wants you, I'm sure he knows how to get you. Don't play yourself with those thoughts." She laughed in the phone.

"I'm going to allow you to believe what you're saying, but you know as well as I, that you're not who he wants. If you were, he wouldn't have you shacked up in some sleazy hotel, which I'm sure you are." I didn't say a word.

"Has he taken you shopping yet?" This bitch was getting on my nerves.

"Your silence tells me all I need to know. Let me break it down for you, whoever you are."

"Dreek, is a rare breed and it's hard to get him to not only love, but trust you. The shopping trips and hotel stays are nothing. When you've seen the inside of his home, not condo, but his real home, met his mother, daughter, friends, and he sleeps with you without protection, then claim you're that bitch.

Until then, play your position of the jump-off you are and don't answer his phone again."

"Bitch when I find out who you are."

"It's no secret boo. My name is?-" I never heard what she said.

"Yo, are you on my phone?" I turned around as Dreek came in the room with food in his hand.

"It rang."

"So the fuck what bitch. Don't ever think its ok to touch any of my stuff. Matter of fact, you just fucked up. Get your shit, so I can take your ass home." I heard laughter coming from the phone. He snatched it from me and looked at it.

"Yo, where you at?" I walked over to see what food he had.

"Hello. Hello." She must've hung up and it infuriated him more. Maybe she's right about him only wanting her.

"DREEKKKKKKKK!" I screamed out as I felt my hair being ripped out my scalp.

"Don't ever touch my shit." The blow to my face was powerful and so was the kick to my chest. Whoever this chick is had him in a rage when she hung up. I had to hurry up and find her, to get rid of her. I damn sure don't need her interfering and having him beat me like this.

★★★★★★★★★★★★★★★

"So bitchhhhhhh. How is it being with Dreek? You should hook me up with Percy. His ass can get it." My best friend Rah Asia said. Me, her and this other chick named Samantha, have been best friends for some years now.

She was there when my ex Brandon cheated on me with the bitch he ended up marrying. For a long time, I assumed it was my then, best friend Jiao. I saw the way he looked and lusted after her. She never paid it any mind and came to me on a few occasions and told me he tried to sleep with her. However, being young and in love I believed him over her, which caused us not to be friends.

She beat my ass a few times over it because I came for her more than once with the bullshit. I should've known our friendship meant more to her than a nigga. Thinking about it all

108

now, she always had my back and never gave me a reason to believe him, but again, I was young and learned my lesson.

Now I have a seven-year-old son with his stupid ass that he took from me, and I see him when he allows. The reason he has my son is because after he left me for the chick he married, I was homeless and my mom wouldn't let me live with her. She told me to leave him alone and I didn't listen, so she held a grudge.

Before I lost him, I did get a job and my son went to day care everyday with no help from Brandon. However, he went behind my back and filed for custody. At the time, my son and I were sleeping in a motel that I paid $150 a week for. It had a kitchen, bathroom and bed, which is all we needed at the time.

The judge still saw me as unfit and placed him with his dad. To this day, I believe Brandon paid the judge off because as long as I had stability, he should have never been allowed to take him.

His wife and I speak about my son only and a few times almost came to blows over her having my son call her mom. I could see if I didn't see or take care of him, but I did, so I was very unhappy with the shit. Brandon told me I was overreacting but how?

It's ok though because in a couple weeks, we have to go to family court and with the money I've gotten from Dreek, I now have an apartment and a car. My job just promoted me to manager so I'm good.

"I can try but Percy seems to be all into his baby momma." I told her and stuck a fry in my mouth. I've met Dreek's friend but he never had a smile on his face. It was as if he despised me and I didn't know why.

"How about right now?" She pointed to Dreek and Percy walking in the food court of the mall. I wasn't sure if I should speak because we haven't since he damn near killed me over answering his phone.

"Hey Dreek. What up Percy?" Rah Asia flirted. She is such a ho, I swear.

"What's up? Come here Mandy." I stood up and made my way to him.

"Hey." I played shy.

"Have your pussy ready for me later."

"Umm. Ok."

"I'll text you the hotel information." He smacked me on the ass and sent me on my way like a kid.

"I'll be waiting for your call." I heard Rah Asia say to Percy.

"You got his number?" I asked and sat down.

"No, he has mine though. I told him I wanted to fuck and he was down."

"Really."

"Yup. If he's into his baby momma like you said, ain't no need to try and make him my man." She shrugged her shoulders.

I hope she knew what she was getting into. I had the same attitude in the beginning fucking Dreek and look where I'm at now. In love with a man, who will probably never see me as more than a jump-off.

Sommer

"Got damn baby, you feel good." Percy moaned as I rode him in his favorite position; cowgirl style.

"I'm cumming Percy."

"Let it go Sommer." He reached over and began massaging my already engorged clit.

"Fuck, I'm cumming with you." He held my waist and most likely got me pregnant again.

Unfortunately for him, my ass planned this sex and had the plan b under the bathroom sink. I wish I would have another kid with him, knowing he's fucking other bitches. He thinks I'm stupid, but every woman knows when your man starts getting late night phone calls, comes in the house at different hours and spends more time accusing you of doing what the fuck he is, somethings going on.

I should be using protection but I know damn well he ain't that stupid to sex them without a condom. I can't really say much because we never gave each other the title of being girlfriend/ boyfriend but he won't dare allow me to entertain another man, yet, he's doing it with other women.

I hopped up and went to take a shower or so he thought. I heard his phone going off the entire time we were having sex. I could have addressed it but I'm the type of woman who would rather catch you red handed then make accusations he'll deny.

I let the shower run and did get in but I never turned it off when I finished. Percy knew I took long showers; especially after sex to get the sticky feeling off. I stood by the door and listened to him attempt to whisper to whom I'm assuming is the chick he's sleeping with. He told her she had no business calling this late and he'd see her tomorrow. You know the usual, let me go before my girl gets out the shower. Little did he know, I was already done.

"Hey, who was that calling this late?" I chuckled quietly as the lie of it being Dreek rolled off his tongue.

"I'm going to be out all day tomorrow. If you need me, I'll make sure to answer and if I can't, hit Dreek."

"Oh, you won't be together?" I questioned.

"Nah. He has some things going on too but he'll be more available than I will."

"Ok. Goodnight." I put my pajamas on and went in the other room with my daughter.

See we haven't really been having sex since the shit with Chrissy. We may have kissed here and there but sex wasn't an option. I only gave in tonight because I wanted him to think we had no issues when I followed his ass tomorrow. I planned on waking up super early, dropping Raven off to Jiao and spend the day seeing what or who is so important that he had to lie.

****

I woke up early like I said, got Raven and I dressed, rushed to drop her off and drove back to Percy's house. I was in Jiao's car so he wouldn't realize it was me following him. No one knew the ride she had, so it made perfect sense to use it. In my heart, I didn't want to stoop this low and should let the evidence fall in my lap, but I needed to see for myself. It's like my gut told me he's sleeping around but I won't feel content until I catch him.

"Hey bitch. Did you catch him yet?" Jiao asked when she called me.

"Bitch, I just left. I'm sitting outside the house now. Wait! Here he comes. Why the fuck is he up and out this early anyway? I'll call you back."

I hung up with her and waited for him to pull out the driveway. It took us almost twenty minutes to get to whoever's house this was. He knocked on the door and when the chick opened it, she fell in his embrace and the two of them began kissing. My heart literally broke in two.

As I cried, I did what most women do and snapped some pictures on my phone. He'll never tell me I'm bugging or imagining shit. You know men say those words a lot when you catch them out there. They usually get away with it when there's no proof, but I got it, so I'm good.

I sat outside the house for a good two hours before any signs of life came out. Percy opened the door and the chick only had on a short robe, barely covering her ass. She walked him to the car and he stood her in front of him. Again, they kissed and this dirty nigga had the nerve to finger pop her outside.

The shit unfolding in front of me had my insides boiling. Of course, I had to be smart and call his phone. He glanced down at it and so did she. She tried to snatch it out his hand and he tossed her against the car. I couldn't hear anything he said but by the looks of it, he was letting her have it.

I waited a few minutes and she started rubbing on his chest, I guess trying to make him forgive her. The shit is funny because he's going to come home and pretend none of this even occurred. I dialed his number again and watched him send me to voicemail. Is she really important enough to ignore me?

The crazy part is, his phone must've rung again because he put it to his ear and started talking. Whatever was said, he hung up, kissed the chick and smacked her on the ass before getting in his car.

Now as the woman who literally fucked him last night, I felt had the right to knock on the bitch's door. However, lucky for her, I had enough information and footage to do what

116

I needed to. She will be dealt with later if necessary. I say if necessary because if he leaves her alone after I find out, she'll come for me like most side chick/mistresses do and I'll beat the shit out of her.

"Hey babe. You called?" Percy asked. He called me ten minutes after he left and tried to have a conversation with me, but I shut shit down.

"Sommer, I told you last night, I'd be unavailable at times today."

"Ok. But if I'm calling you back to back something could've been wrong. Anyway, why were you out the house so early?" The phone was silent. I had to check and make sure he was still on it.

"Are you ok?"

"Oh. Ugh yea. I had to handle something."

"Ok. Well, I'm going to let you go because it seems like you're aggravated and I don't want to fight with you."

"Why did you call?"

"It doesn't matter now. If it did, you would've answered."

117

CLICK! I hung up on him and like clockwork, he called right back. I turned my phone off and headed to Jiao's.

I immediately broke down when she opened the door. I mean the ugly cry came out along with the snot and drool. I loved Percy with all my heart but he was doing some foul shit. Now before anyone talks shit, we may not have the title but we did everything a couple did. We went out on dates, he catered to me, spent nights home alone cuddling and everything else that came along with being a couple. The only thing we didn't do was sex and it happened last night.

He wouldn't allow me to speak to any dudes and barely wanted me to leave for work. Yet, here he is sleeping around and pretending things were great.

"What happened?" I told Jiao and she became upset too. The two of us are like frick and frack. When one hurts, so does the other.

"Sommer, I'm going to keep it real with you." I nodded. I already knew what she was about to say because I've said the same thing to her about Dreek.

"Percy and you are not a couple. Yes, you live together, have a daughter and act like one, but the fact remains; you're not. You have every right to be upset, but you're playing a part in it too."

"What you mean?"

"You're staying in his house, acting like a couple, sleeping in the same bed, sex or not and listening to what he says about not being with anyone else. Now if you're not happy, then leave. I know it's easier said than done, but if you don't plan on being with him, it has to be this way or he'll continue to do it and you'll always be mad."

"I want Raven to grow up with him."

"She will and don't use her as an excuse to stick around. If he's going to sleep with others, he'll do it whether you're there or not. He isn't respecting what y'all have and it's up to you to make changes. Now what are you going to do?"

She passed me some tissues and sat next to me feeding Raven. I stared at my daughter and thought about how I would never want her hurting the way I am. Could I allow her to grow up thinking her mom is weak?

"Fine. I'm moving in here with you. Dree is going to have to share her room."

"Good luck with that. You know she called and said since her daddy won't let her see me, she wants a lock on her door. I said for what? She had the nerve to say because I don't want anyone in there." We both busted out laughing.

"There's a full-size bed in lil Dreek's room. You can stay in there."

"Hell no. I am not staying in your son's room."

"Girl please. He'll be in my bed anyway."

"Fine but its only until I find someplace else."

I hadn't been staying in my own place because Kevin had been stalking me. After the baby shower, somehow, he got my number and sent me a bunch of threatening, love and hateful messages. He had some serious issues going on and I'm staying as far away as possible. Don't ask how he found out where I lived.

I stayed over her house for a few hours and decided it was time to go home and face the music. Percy wasn't there, so it gave me time to pack and get myself together. I knew with it being late, I didn't want to take the chance of leaving tonight and he catch me, because his ass would fight me tooth and nail. I packed and put most of my things in my trunk. He wouldn't see it and in the morning, I'd be gone. I bathed me and my daughter, got in the bed and prepared myself for the heartache I knew would come.

Percy

"If Sommer finds out, you know she's leaving, right?" Dreek said as we sat in VIP of the club. I've been out the house all day and the only time I spoke with Sommer was when she called my phone earlier.

"I know but Rah Asia is a freak and man; the bitch lets me do any and everything to her." He shook his head laughing.

"But is she worth losing Sommer over?"

"That's the thing. I'm not trying to lose Sommer, but at the same time, she and I aren't a couple either."

"Are you serious?" I looked at him.

"Nigga, you won't allow Sommer to mess with anyone else. She lives with you, cooks, cleans, fucks, sucks and takes good care of your kids. She's dealt with the Chrissy bullshit and stayed around after you played her at the baby shower. A title doesn't mean you aren't together."

"Who are you, Dr. Phil and when did you become a love expert?"

"Nigga, don't knock my new job." We both started laughing.

"I'm saying all that freaky shit, you can get Sommer to do, plus you know shorty a ho."

"I know, but a nigga done fucked around and caught feelings for her."

"I should punch you in the face for Sommer. What the fuck is wrong with you? Did you not learn anything from what I went through with Jiao? Shit, she had my head gone and I'm just now starting to get it together." He was in love with her but I think the longer she's gone, it's easier for him to move on.

"Look, I'm not judging you because I'm the last nigga who should say anything but let Sommer go. She's gone through a lot to be with you and in return, you shitting on her. The least you can do is save face and make it seem like it's not working. If she finds out about Rah Asia, it's going to be hell to pay." I nodded.

He was right, I needed to let Sommer go. However, I didn't want to. Call me stingy, selfish or whatever but Sommer was and still is the woman I want to marry.

123

Rah Asia is not someone I wanted to make my woman. Yea, she does a lot of freaky things but there's no love for her. I caught feelings but not the kind to make me want to wife her. The type of feelings I caught are more like lust. She does whatever I say and lets me fuck on demand. Shit, Sommer and I have only had sex twice since the shit happened with my ex and a nigga was horny. I could have waited but then again, like I said before, we are not a couple.

After a few more drinks, Dreek and I parted ways. I took my ass home and looked at my phone to block Rah Asia. Last night her stupid ass kept calling while I was with Sommer. I need to get my head right before I get too caught up with this chick and lose out on the best woman I've ever had. Not to mention, I'll never allow her to date another nigga anyway. I guess my fun is over and I'll make it to Rah Asia tomorrow and let her know too.

"What up?" I walked in the house and spoke to Sommer who was coming out the kitchen with a bottle for my daughter.

"Hey. How was your day?" She had a smirk on her face.

124

"Tiring. You good." I could see something was wrong but I won't address it until I get out the shower. I washed over Rah Asia's house but after being out all day, I needed to wash again.

"Never been better." I didn't respond and went upstairs to clean up. When I came out, I expected her to be in the bed. I put on my basketball shorts and went to find her.

"How's my baby girl doing?" I picked Raven up out of her hands and held her. I loved the hell out of my kids and the only stability they had, was me and Sommer.

"I'm sorry." I told her and she nodded her head and continued to watch television. I wanted to say I was sorry for not answering her earlier, sleeping with another woman and anything else I messed up on but the words wouldn't come out when I noticed some of Raven's things were missing.

"Where's Raven's diapers, wipes and other things that are usually on the changing table? And her swing isn't here either." She never spoke a word and walked out the room. I figured she moved the stuff in one of the extra rooms so I left it alone.

I put Raven to bed and checked on Percy Jr. who was in his room knocked out. I turned the television off and instead of taking my ass to bed like I should have, I went in my room, picked my phone up and called Rah Asia. It wasn't on no disrespectful shit, it was to tell her we were through. Something about the way Sommer stared at me and ignored my questions had me wondering if she was going to leave me.

"Hey baby. I missed you."

"Rah Asia listen."

"Guess what?" She said happily in the phone.

"What?"

"I think I'm pregnant." I sat there in silence.

"Percy, you there?"

"If you are, get rid of it."

"WHAT?" She was now yelling in the phone.

"You heard me. I messed up one time and you promised to take the pill."

"But I thought you loved me."

"Bitch, are you crazy? The only person I love is Sommer."

126

"Don't start with that bitch again."

"Yo, you way out of line. In the beginning, I told you, this was nothing but a fuck. Yea, we've been doing it a lot, but never did I say, you could speak on her."

"Percy, this isn't your choice."

"Who put the baby in you?" She didn't answer.

"Who put the fucking baby in you?" I asked in a loud whisper. I was trying not to yell because I damn sure didn't want Sommer to hear this.

"You did."

"Exactly. Therefore, it is my choice too, regardless if it's in your body. What type of shit are you trying to prove?"

"I'm not getting rid of it." She hung the phone up and my temper got the best of me.

I threw a shirt and my sneakers on, grabbed my keys and ran down the steps. My car couldn't get me there fast enough. My phone started going off but I ignored it. I parked in front of Rah Asia's house and banged on her door. She tried to give me a key previously, but I wouldn't take it.

"Percy, why are you?"

127

I snatched her up by the neck and drug her in the kitchen. I held onto her, opened the cabinet under the sink and rummaged through the cleaners. This bitch had me twisted if she thought for one second, she'd have my kid. I found what I was looking for and sat her ass in the chair. I could see how scared she was but everyone knew the type of niggas we were. Yes, my boy is ten times worse but a nigga like me, will get it popping too.

"Percy, what are you doing?" I twisted the cap off and poured it in a cup.

"You know exactly what I'm doing."

"I'll get rid of it. Please don't make me drink that."

"Nah. You were tough on the phone. Talking shit like it was cool. This will let me know the job is done."

"What if I die?'

"Not my problem. Open your fucking mouth." She refused and made me drop the cup.

"Oh, we're going to do this the hard way."

I squeezed her cheeks and poured the bleach from the bottle down her throat. She fought, scratched and kicked. It didn't matter because the bleach was going down. She began choking but I never stopped pouring.

After the bottle was empty she laid there trying to make herself vomit. I grabbed a bottle of pine sol, twisted the cap, did the same thing and watched her cry. Yea, it's my fault she's pregnant but I'll be damned if she makes the choice to keep it on her own.

I grabbed a water out the fridge to drink and stood there staring at her body convulse. Her eyes were bulging and foam came from her mouth. I should feel bad, however, all I cared about right now was making things right with Sommer. I lifted my phone off my waist to make a call to Dreek and got the shock of my life when I read the message.

My wife: *Going to your new bitch huh? I really hope she was worth it. We won't be here when you return. The nanny is her with Percy Jr."* How the fuck did she find out. After I read the message, I scrolled through the photos and the video of me finger fucking Rah Asia outside her house. I was not only stupid for sleeping with this ho, but carless as fuck.

"Yo." Dreek answered right away. I guess he would being its after one in the morning.

"I need someone to mop the floor over this chick's house. She can't clean for shit." I spoke in code about sending someone in to handle Rah Asia.

"You need to pick cleaner bitches." He laughed and hung up. I sent him the address and rushed to my house.

"SOMMER." I yelled out when I opened the door.

"She's not here Mr. Miller. Is everything ok?" My nanny asked.

"When did she leave?"

"Ummm, about ten minutes ago."

"FUCKKK!" I locked the door and went upstairs to my room.

"The number you reached is no longer in service, please hang up and try your call again." Is what the operator said each time I dialed the number. I don't know why my ass thought the message would change. Once you get a new number, the old one goes to someone else. How the fuck am I going to find her or my daughter?

130

Jiao

"Wake up sis." I heard and felt someone shaking me. I reached for the lamp on the night stand and turned it on.

"Hey. Are you ok?" Shaky stood in front of me with tears running down her face. I moved my covers back and slid over so she could get in with me.

"What happened?" She started running down the shit with Percy coming in the house late pretending everything was good and how he ran out in the middle of the night. She overheard him on the phone with some chick and how he wanted her to get rid of something. We put two and two together, and guess she's probably pregnant.

"Where's Raven?"

"In the room sleep. I don't know what to do J. He's going to be looking for me and Kevin has been stalking me everyday."

"What you mean? I thought your dad found him."

"So did I but when he sent people in to get Kevin, he was gone. My dad said it's like someone told him."

"Who?" She shrugged her shoulders and we laid there not saying a word.

"No idea." She wiped her eyes and got off the bed.

I followed her out the room and made sure the door downstairs was locked. Call me crazy but it's what I do. For some reason, I opened it and scanned the parking lot for Sommer's car. No one knows I'm here but if he looks for and sees her car, he'll knock on every door. Percy cannot know where I am, because he for sure will tell his friend. I did notice a car that looked similar to Dreek's. I threw a hat on, closed my door a little and walked to it.

"Jiao, what are you doing?" I heard Sommer yell in a whisper. I turned around and she was speed walking towards me.

"Is this Dreek's car?" I asked when she caught up.

"I don't know. Bitch, it's late and why do you care if it is?" I shrugged. We got to the car and I looked inside.

"Fuck! Who lives here?" I started panicking.

The day I left Sommer's parents' house, this is where I had been staying. It's a half hour from Dreek and close enough for his mom to drop Dree off, well before anyway. Now it seems as if he were staying here or at least visiting someone, but who could it be? Is this where he creeps off to when he doesn't have Dree and does she know? I hope she never mentioned this spot to him.

"Jiao, is that your old cell phone and car keys?" Sommer asked with her face to the window.

"Yea. It's how I knew it was his car once we walked up on it."

"Why you think he has it?"

"Who knows?" He's been to the old house and from what her dad told me, he has someone watching it.

"Give me something to scratch this bitch."

"What? Hell no J. He loves this car and I will not be a part of your madness" I tried my luck and opened the door to find it unlocked. I took my keys out and walked all around the car, scratching the hell out of it. Call me petty all you want but he deserves this and so much more.

I opened the pocket knife I had attached to my key ring and stuck it in his tires. The hissing sound was loud but not enough to wake anyone up. I thought about busting the windows out but it would wake him up and I wouldn't have enough time to get back to his house. I continued fucking the car up as much as possible. I keyed the words, Fuck nigga, Manwhore, and some other shit on the hood.

A light came on as I placed the car keys back in the car. If I took them, he may know it was me and go on an even worse manhunt to find me. We walked back to my house slow and kept looking behind us.

When we got in the house and locked the door, we both fell on the couch cracking up. Sommer is my ride or die and a bitch definitely appreciated her being here. After talking about how he was going to be pissed in the morning, I took my ass back to bed with a huge smile on my face.

****

"Bitchhhhhhhh, look at him." Sommer had me peeking out the door. I saw Percy, Bash, Jaime and a few other people standing there. However, I didn't expect to see Queenie. She had on some short ass shorts, with a tank top and a small robe. Dreek would kick my ass if I came to the door like that. *I think.*

"What you think he saying?" I asked.

"He's probably trying to figure out which bitch he fucking did it." I noticed Jaime turn and look in our direction. We both waved and he put his head down laughing.

"Shut the door sis." I told her and went to my room to get dressed. I had a doctor's appointment and then we were going to Jersey Garden's mall.

The doctor appointment went fine. She told me I was seven and a half months now and needed to start prepping for delivery. She didn't say I was going early, but I needed to get me and the baby's hospital bag ready. All last-minute things like a crib, stroller, car seat and things a baby will need right away, should be purchased and put together now. She also said sex is a good thing and it will help with the delivery.

Unfortunately, it's not happening. I left the office with a big grin on my face. It was almost time to meet my son and I couldn't be happier. Sommer parked in the expected mothers parking lot of the mall and I took Raven out the seat as she got the stroller out the trunk.

"Hey ladies." Dreek's mom spoke and Dree came running to me.

"Oh my God! How did you get her out the house?" I knew his mom would meet us here but she never mentioned bringing Dree.

"He said something happened to his car and asked me to take her shopping to make up for him missing their date. They were going to the movies and then out for lunch. I think she'd rather be here anyway." Dree asked to push Raven in the stroller as we walked in. Dree is going to be such a great big sister.

"You think he'll enjoy this?" I heard behind me in Victoria Secrets.

Say what you want but they have the best smelling lotions out. I used to get the cucumber melon from Bath and Body works but they no longer sell them in the store. I had an entire box of them at home from buying them online but the vanilla lace smelled better from here.

"Dreek don't care what you have on." All of us stopped to see who it was. When she turned around, I could have spit in

136

her face. I know damn well he didn't stoop low and fuck with her.

"Hey Jiao. How are you?"

"Why you keep acting as if I'm going to speak to you? Like I told you at my mother's funeral.-" I was cut off.

"Jiao, who is she?" I didn't want to expose Dreek's daughter to the bullshit.

"No one honey. Go stand with Sommer." I waited for her to leave.

"Like I was saying."

"You weren't saying shit bitch. Standing here pregnant by some man who probably don't even want your ass. Look at you, fat as a cow, and acting ghetto as hell. Your mom would be proud." When she said that, I hooked off on her. I made sure I didn't let her kick or make me fall on the ground. I continued hitting her over and over until I felt someone lifting me off.

"Jiao, what the hell is going on?" I heard and it was Robert. Shit, he's going to tell Dreek.

"Nothing."

"What you mean nothing?" He looked at Mandy and then my stomach.

"Jiao, you ain't shit yo. He's not going to be happy when he finds out."

"Ma'am, I'm going to have to ask all of you to leave." I turned around and it was security.

"I want her arrested." Mandy yelled out, holding her nose. Security was about to call someone on the radio but Robert stopped him.

"Who fights with a baby in their stomach? Ratchet ass bitches." Mandy's friend said and Sommer jumped on her. It was like people came from everywhere to watch.

"Are you serious?" I heard and turned around to see Dree, kicking Mandy in the back as she sat on the ground. She grabbed Dree by the hair and all I saw was red. I loved my baby and I'm going straight to the emergency room when I leave, but I'm beating her ass right now.

I went to get Mandy but Dreek's mom was rocking the shit out of her. I mean, banging her head in the ground and then she told Dree to come over. When Dree got to her, she made her stomp Mandy in the face.

"CALM THE FUCK DOWN." I heard and froze. I started to walk off and was grabbed from behind.

"Get off me."

"Yo, don't make me fuck you up J." Dreek's voice boomed through my ear.

I turned around and smacked the shit out of Jaime. He played too fucking much. He was a got damn comedian all of a sudden. We told him so many times he sounded like Dreek and could make anyone think he was him behind the scenes.

"Jiao, calm your pregnant ass down."

"Why would you do that?"

"Listen. You need to go. Dreek is in the mall with Percy and he's not in a good mood after what you did to his car."

"Fuck his car and all these dumb ass bitches he fucking."

"Jiao, get the fuck out of here." Jaime said and I noticed Robert looking at him weird.

"Ma, you know better than to have J out here fighting. Look at her." Robert said but still trying to diffuse the situation.

"Ain't no one messing with my daughters or granddaughter." His mom loved me and Sommer and told anyone who asked we are her long lost daughters. She walked up to him.

"You better not mention Jiao was here at all Robert. You know I love you like my son, but I will cut your ass off, if he finds out."

"Really ma."

"Really. Come on y'all." She grabbed Dree's hand and we all went rushing in the other direction.

"Why are you stopping Jiao?" His mom asked.

"Mandy's going to tell."

"I doubt she'll say it was you. She doesn't want anyone to know a pregnant girl an eight-year-old beat her ass." We started laughing and got in the car. Today was a good day.

Dreek

"What the fuck happened to you?" I asked Mandy when I saw her sitting in one of the chairs in the mall. Her nose was bleeding and overall, it looked like someone fucked her up.

"Some chicks just jumped me." I noticed Robert and Jaime both shaking their heads. I'll ask them about it later. She's probably lying.

"I guess you're not a fighter." Percy said laughing and it made me laugh.

"Really Dreek."

"What? Whoever they were, beat the shit out of you. Not everyone will win every fight, but damn, did you even get a pluck, pinch of kick in. You look like shit." I couldn't stop talking shit. Mandy swears she's tough, so to see her beat the fuck up made me laugh and crack jokes.

"I swear, I'm going to get her back once she drops the baby." I stopped laughing when she said it.

"Yo, a pregnant bitch did this to you? I'm fucking done." I started laughing harder and my boys didn't help because they did the same thing. She rolled her eyes.

141

"Ok. How many chicks was it?"

"Three and some little girl."

"So, you let five people beat your ass."

"Five? I said four and they only got over because they jumped me."

"Yea five. It's obvious the baby helped too." I swear the shit was hysterical.

"Damnnnnnnn." We all yelled out when her friend approached.

"You too." Percy asked.

"Fuck y'all. Her ex best friend did this to her. Then the bitch had her friend, their momma and even the little girl get in it. Who the fuck lets a little girl fight?"

"Obviously someone who thought she could beat you. Did the kid hit you too?"

"No. Only the bitch ass friend fought me."

"Yo. I wouldn't tell anyone that. I would say they jumped me too because one chick beat you like the couple who got her." Jaime had jokes for days.

"What you laughing for? You were right here, egging them on." I turned to look at him.

"You saw it yo and didn't tape it? You got to be quicker on your feet with the record button. This the type of shit we laugh at."

"I was too busy laughing."

"Who were the chicks?" He shrugged his shoulders but something told me he knew exactly who it was.

"Dreek can you take me home?"

"HELL NO. You ain't getting blood on my seats and shit. You better get home, the same way you got here." I started walking away.

"He is so ignorant. How do you even lay down with him?" I heard the girl ask.

"Because my dick is big and she loves the way I fuck. What? You want some too?" Mandy's mouth fell open.

"Yuk. I would never fuck my friends man."

"HOLD THE FUCK UP! I KNOW GOT DAMN WELL SHE AIN'T TELL YOU I WAS HER MAN." Mandy stood up and grabbed her things.

143

"Let's go Samantha."

"Mandy, you need to reevaluate if he's worth it. He's nothing but a fucking loser who.-" Is all she got out before I slid her across the ground. Who the fuck did she think she was? I saw a few old people cover their mouths when I did it, but oh fucking well.

"Oh my God Dreek?" I shrugged my shoulders.

"Meet me at the room later. You know the number and don't make me wait." Mandy nodded her head.

"You ain't shit nigga. I would hate to be a female you fucked with." Jaime said as we walked in the store.

"These bitches stupid, that's why the only one who I could rock with was Jiao. She gave me a run for my money but she also didn't take my shit. I need some discipline in my life. These bitches are beyond weak."

"Yo, get the hell out of here." Percy said laughing.

"Who you getting these Jordan's for?" I asked Jaime. He didn't have a girl and he never told us about a baby.

"My godson, bro. Damn. Back up."

"What the fuck ever? If it were my son, I'd get him these." I felt myself getting upset about Jiao losing him. Queenie still didn't know what she's having and I ain't buying the bitch a damn thing until I'm sure it's my baby.

"These it is then. I'll make sure to let his mom know you picked them out."

"Well shit, since he's your godson and probably going to be around us, I'm going to get him these two pair too and a few of these Jordan outfits to match." Baby stores these days had a ton of shit for kids and they weren't as expensive.

All of us stayed at the mall for a few hours buying shit and then eating in the food court. I felt my phone vibrating on my waist and pulled it out the clip. I noticed the number was unknown, which meant it's probably Jiao. I moved away from the guys and went to the other side of the food court to answer.

"Where I'm meeting you at?"

"Still rude as fuck. Hello would have been fine." I had to smile. She always tried to put me in my place.

"Time and place."

"About that. Dreek."

145

"Don't even try it J. I asked Sommer to set it up a over a month ago. I gave you your space but you're trying the shit out of me. Especially, fucking with my car the way you did."

"I don't know what you're talking about."

"Next time you try and mess with someone's car try not to leave shit behind."

"What are you talking about? I didn't leave anything there. Fuck!" She gave herself away. She didn't leave anything and I was testing her to see if it were her and got my answer.

"Whatever. Where you want to meet?"

"You gave in pretty easy. I expected to threaten and come find you first."

"You make me sick."

"I know."

"I'm going to rent a room at the Double Tree."

"J, we can meet somewhere else." I remembered her telling me that's the hotel her mom was murdered in. I may be an asshole but I wouldn't dare ask for her to return there.

"I'm ok Dreek, but thank you for being concerned."

"I'm not concerned. I just.-"

146

"Dreek it's me. You don't have to be tough for me." I hated she knew me so well.

"Whatever. What time?"

"I'll be there in two hours. If you're a second late, I'm gone and you better not fucking keep Dree from me."

"Alright damn." I hung up and walked back to the boys. I stopped when I noticed the dude with Charlotte was the same guy who ruined Sommer's baby shower but why were they together? I didn't have time to worry about it right now.

"I'm out yo. J, called and she's going to meet me."

"I'm coming." Jaime said and stood up.

"For what nigga?"

"Man, ain't nobody about to let your hostile ass see her alone." Percy agreed with Jaime.

"I'm not going to kill her. I need to know what went down with her and my brother."

"BULLSHIT!" All of them shouted.

"Whatever." I don't need an entourage. Thanks, but no thanks." I chucked the deuces up and bounced. I had to run home and change clothes. I can't even lie; a nigga is happy as

147

hell to see her. I parked in front of my house and sent my mom a text to tell her Dree was staying the night. Once she confirmed, I went to clean up.

"I'm here." J spoke in the phone. I looked at the time and noticed I had a half hour to get there. I put my clothes on and hauled ass to the hotel.

I made my way in the hotel, walked past the desk and straight to the elevator. I pressed the button and took it to the fourth floor. The doors opened and I stepped off and heard yelling. I ran in the direction of the room and pushed the door opened. Her father stood there and turned when he noticed me.

For some reason, he put his head down and walked out the room. What in the hell is going on with him? When she introduced us at the restaurant, I admit he had a familiar look as well but until I put it together, I won't say anything.

"J." I walked up on her as she sat on the couch. She never turned around when I walked in. She was sniffling and her head was down.

"Why you crying?" I touched her shoulder.

"I'm sorry Dreek."

"Sorry for what?" I made my way around the couch.

"Yo, you good?" I heard and saw Jaime, Robert and Percy coming in. I shook my head at their crazy ass. I didn't even bother to make them leave.

"What are you sorry for J?" She removed a pillow from her lap, stood up and my anger immediately took over. My hands were around her throat so fast, no one had time to stop me.

Jiao

I dug my nails in Dreek's arms as he continued choking me. I saw my life flash before my eyes and blamed myself. I was being selfish and kept this secret, when it was my responsibility to tell him. Jaime knew and once Dreek found out about it, he's going to probably kill him. I made my bed and now I must lie in it, but not before I hit his ass back.

"Get off her." I heard his mom say and it snapped him out of the trance he was in. At this very moment, I was glad I called her over. I knew when he saw me, he'd flip but not this bad.

WHAP! I smacked the shit out of him. Then followed it up with a few punches to his face. I knew he wouldn't be able to get me back with everyone standing there so I pushed my luck.

"That's enough Jiao? I may have let you lay hands on him but you're not about to overdue it." His mom said. I understood because at the end of the day, she's his mom and isn't about to let anyone put hands on her son. I'm going to be the same way, so I get it.

"I'm out." They let him go and he came to stand in front of me.

"Whose baby is that?" I went to swing. He caught my arm.

"If you even think about kicking me or breaking my finger again, I'll have this baby cut out and kill you." The way he said it, sent chills down my spine.

"I'm going to ask you again. Who's baby is it?"

"Yours."

"When you have it, I want a test."

"WHAT?"

"You've been away from me for too long and let's not forget the fact you told me, you lost it. Get out your fucking feelings and deal with the shit you had me believing."

"Dreek, I said I was sorry." He let my hands go.

"You're sorry. Huh?" He chuckled.

"Sorry don't fix this shit J. Not this time. Don't say a fucking word to me until the baby's born." He opened the hotel door and turned around.

"All you motherfuckers knew."

"I ain't no shit bro. You know I would've told you." Percy said and gave Jiao a hateful stare.

"Dreek, I found out at the mall earlier." Robert explained.

"And you Jaime? Is those who the sneakers are for?" When he didn't answer Dreek charged him but his mom stood in the way.

"I asked Jaime not to tell you son."

"Ma, you too."

"Jaime told me and Jiao on plenty of occasions, he wasn't comfortable keeping this from you. He threatened to tell you but we kept telling him, she would tell you. Don't be mad at him." I stood in the room staring at everyone. How could I be so close with them and they keep my secret? I guess his friends were mine too.

"Dreek, I wanted to tell you." I walked over to him.

"I called you because Bash told me I had to tell you."

"Everybody fucking knew but me. What the fuck?"

"Dreek, I called and Queenie answer and I heard you threaten to kill me on sight. What did you expect me to do?"

"I expected you to mention it J. I don't care what the fuck I said. Do you have any idea what I went through thinking you lost this baby? DO YOU?" I started crying.

"I had a got damn tattoo on my fucking shoulder with the death of a son, I supposedly didn't lose." He showed it to me and they all looked. I guess he never told them either.

"You know J. No other woman could ever say she made me fall in love or even miss her the way I did when it came to you. I told you a long time ago, I never saw myself jumping in front of a bullet for anyone besides my mother and daughter but you came into my life and changed that. I would go to war with anyone for fucking with you and I think you know it. Now, I could care less what the fuck happens to you."

"Dreek." I grabbed his arm and he gave me a look. I let go and backed away. He lifted my face and stared at the scratch under my eye.

"Did you fight Mandy earlier?" I nodded my head.

"Keep her away from me and Dree."

"Andreek Puryear." His mom yelled.

"Ma, I know you love her as your own but I won't allow her or any woman around my daughter who has her fighting in a fucking mall."

"Dreek, she grabbed Dree's hair and.-"

"I don't give a fuck what the bitch did. If you weren't fighting, it never would have happened. You of all people know how Dree is and she won't let anyone fuck with you. My daughter worships the ground you walk on J and this sneaky shit you have her caught up in, ain't what it is. And before you say shit, she hasn't been and won't ever be around Queenie again. I made sure of it because you were right saying I should've kept Dree away from her a long time ago. I also knew you would have a fit and I didn't want to hear your mouth."

"Dreek, I'm sorry but don't keep Dree from me. Please."

"Why not? You kept this baby from me?" He said and walked out with his boys behind him.

"I told you this would happen J. Now I got to hear him curse me the fuck out over it. Make this shit right." Jaime said.

"I don't know how."

"Figure it out." He pointed to a bag from the mall.

"Dreek picked everything out, thinking it was for my godson." He left and I plopped down on the couch, put my knees to my chest and cried.

"He'll be fine J." His mom said and had me stand up.

"I don't know ma." I asked if I could call her that and she told me to make sure I'm not trying to replace my mom because she wasn't having it. I've grown to love her like my own though so I'm glad she said yes..

"The hurt in his eyes and listening to him, says different. I'm never supposed to hurt him. Why didn't I tell him?"

"J, let's get you home. We can worry about it another time. Right now, you need to relax." We grabbed everything and left the hotel.

****

It's been a few weeks since Dreek found out about the pregnancy. I called him that night from my phone and didn't block the number. When he heard my voice, he hung up. I call every day and I know he sees it because he never blocked me. The nights I saw his car down the parking lot, Sommer stopped me from going over there. He may not know where I'm staying but he should at least talk to me.

"You ok sis?" Sommer was still hiding out with me and now she had two niggas stalking her. Percy hadn't seen Raven since the night she left and he was bugging. The messages he left were as bad as the ones Kevin left.

"I'm ok. I miss him Sommer." She sat next to me on the couch.

"Honey, you haven't seen him in a while."

"I know but now that I have and hurt him, I want to make it better."

"Give him time J. He thought you lost his son and most likely blamed himself." I nodded and rubbed my belly. I had two weeks left before I delivered. I heard a knock at the door and prayed it was Dreek. Maybe someone told him where we stayed.

"Hey." He spoke and closed the door.

"How is he?" I asked Bash who called and asked if he could stop by and discuss what went down with my mom. At first, I didn't want to but it's time to find out the truth.

"You know Dreek. He's handling business as if nothing is bothering him."

"Can you set it up so I can see him?"

"Absolutely not. You won't have me caught up." I told him I understood and offered him a seat. Sommer came in with Raven and joined us.

"And you better talk to Percy. His ass ain't wrapped to tight either. He snapping on motherfuckers because you disappeared with his daughter. Y'all got some looney niggas, so I suggest you get used to their behavior." He shrugged his arms like it was normal.

"Tell me what went down at the hotel." I asked trying to take my mind off Dreek."

I sat there listening to him tell how my father cheated on my mom, over and over. He met her at the restaurant a few times and she explained what she was going through. At night, they would speak on the phone for hours and eventually they went on a date, vacations and fell in love. At first, I told him he was lying. He showed me photos of him and my mom on his phone. I was surprised he still had them. She looked so happy and carefree.

He explained that the night of her murder, he went to see her and someone had shot her before he arrived. He tried to take her to the hospital but she wouldn't allow him to. Her main focus was me having the perfect image of her. I asked if she told him who shot her and he said no.

After talking more, we both apologized. Me for shooting him and him for getting her killed. I told him it wasn't his fault but he insisted if he weren't with her, she'd be alive. I couldn't argue with that but it made me feel some way towards my father. Is it why he had little remorse and tears at the funeral? Did he know she was cheating? Could he have been the one to kill her? No. He loved my mom to death, however, someone did. I wonder if it were the guy who came to see her all the times in the restaurant. I heard the oven timer in the kitchen and went to turn it off.

"Did your water break?" Sommer asked when I stood up.

"I don't feel any pain. Maybe, I had an accident."

"Yo, that's nasty as hell. How you not know you peed on yourself?" He is definitely Dreek's brother. Neither of them had any damn filter.

I stuck my finger up at him and told both of them I was taking a shower. If my water did break, I needed to shower before going to the hospital to check. Sommer told me after she gave birth, they wouldn't let her take one right away.

On the way to the hospital there was no pain. I asked Bash not to call anyone yet. Of course, he asked if I learned my lesson from what went down a few weeks ago. I did, but why call him when he wanted a DNA?

The nurses wheeled me up to the labor floor, took my vitals and said the doctor would be in shortly. Sommer didn't come because she was too scared Percy would show up.

After being here for an hour, the doctor finally came in to check and told me, my water broke and I was indeed in the early stages of labor. He had the nurse started prepping for delivery and told me I was only at four centimeters but they were getting ready. When he was on his way out, I asked if he could shut the light off.

I rolled on my side and stared at the machine. I could hear my baby's heartbeat on the monitor. I'll be delivering my son soon and couldn't wait to welcome him in the world.

I felt a presence behind me and was scared to death to turn around. I knew it was him by the scent of cologne he wore. It was my favorite and I wonder if he wore it to come here. Whatever the case, I'm going to curse Bash out for telling him.

Dreek

After I bounced from the hotel that night, I went home alone and had a long talk with myself. I contemplated killing Mandy for fighting Jiao while she was pregnant and putting hands on my daughter. I wasn't sure it was them at first, until J confirmed it.

Who puts their hand on a kid anyway? Mandy explained she didn't grab Dree's hair and was trying to stop her from kicking. Don't ask me how Mandy's hand ended up in Dree's hair though. I tried to see Mandy a few times but she keeps having an excuse on why she can't, which is why I was on my way to her apartment now. I may not be the best father but no bitch will lay hands on her, ever.

"Yo." I answered when I pulled up at Mandy's.

"She's in labor." Bash said in the phone. I knew he was speaking of J, because no one fucked with Queenie.

"What you telling me for? Call me when she delivers."

"Dreek, I know you're upset, trust me, I would be too. I'm not excusing anything she did but you know as well as I,

161

that's your son. Don't miss out on him being born because you're mad."

"I'm busy yo." I hung up and made my way to Mandy's door and started banging on it.

"Mandy ain't here." The same bitch from the mall said with and attitude and tried to close the door. I pushed it open and walked right in. Shorty had a decent place.

"What the fuck you looking at?" She sucked her teeth.

"Look shorty. It's obvious you want to fuck me. How long before your girl gets home?"

"What? No, I don't." She said smiling. I raised my eyebrow at her.

"In a half hour."

"Good, come suck me off first and I'll break you off." She hesitated but then came to where I sat. She unbuckled my jeans, had me lift up and pulled them and my boxers down.

"Oh shit girl." She put me in her mouth and started doing some crazy shit to me, but it felt good as hell. I pumped in and out of her.

162

"Mmmm, you taste good." I had to chuckle at this grimy bitch. Not only is she Mandy's friend but I slid her ass in the mall and she still wanted the D. Like I always say, bitches ain't shit.

"Samantha, can you help me out with these bags?" I heard Mandy say when she opened the door. Shorty ran in the other room and I fixed my clothes. Mandy came in holding bags with her back turned, so she didn't even see me.

"Dreek." She dropped the bag when she looked in my face. I wrapped my hand around her neck and banged her face into the wall.

"Oh my God! Dreek, why are you?" I banged it in the wall again and tossed her on the ground.

"If you ever in your pathetic fucking life lay hands on my daughter or son's mother again, I won't hesitate to kill you." I kicked her in the back and left out the same door I came in.

I know people are wondering why I beat her ass and not Queenie's for fucking with Dree. Queenie may say slick shit to my daughter, roll her eyes or even slip up and curse but she's never laid one hand on her. I've beat Queenie's ass on plenty of occasions when she did but after the time she said fuck you to my daughter, I was done.

Yea, I made her my girlfriend afterwards but I was mad at J. It was stupid and I regret it and broke up with her the night of the party. My mom found out a week later, sat me down and let me have it over that shit.

"Dreek, how you still with a bitch who don't like your daughter?"

"It's my business ma."

"You're right but my grandbaby won't ever be around her again."

"She's not and I apologized to Dree for even putting her in the position to be around such a spiteful person. Dree ain't no saint either but she is a child and Queenie knows better."

"Dreek, I don't get in your business too much but Jiao is the woman you should be with. You both have feelings for each other." I cut her off. My mom has the tendency to go on and on if you let her.

"Ma, I am going to be with her but not right now."

"Why?"

"Hector is up to something and I know its fucked up but I'd rather him think Queenie is my girl, then Jiao. If he comes after me at least he won't bother her."

"That is fucked up Dreek but I understand. Have you told Jiao?"

"Yea but she assumed I was lying and kicked me out her house."

"Maybe it's better that way."

"I said the same thing." I shrugged and we ended up discussing other shit.

I wanted Jiao in my life full time but with Hector, there's no way I could put her in harm's way. Some men don't give a fuck and allow their hearts to lead their significant other straight to their death. I would never forgive myself if something happened to Jiao. It's funny how she assumed her Kung Fu could help keep her safe. I admired her for wanting to say fuck everything so she could be with me, but I'm not built that way.

I walked in the hospital room and stood there staring. Had this been when we were speaking, I'd probably rush to her side. She didn't turn around and I never announced myself. I moved towards the bed and sat in one of the chairs at the foot of it. She rolled over and I heard a bunch of beeping noises and saw some zig zag lines on the monitor. I'm not ignorant to the pain she was experiencing, yet, my ass sat right there. If she wanted me to hold her hand or some shit, she needed to open her mouth.

"Hey Miss Kim. Are you ready for me to check again? Oh, you must be dad." The doctor said and shook my hand. I never responded and let him do what he needed. He lifted the sheet up and stood in front of her as he stuck fingers inside to check. He took them out and pulled the gloves off.

"Ok, Miss Kim. You are about nine centimeters. I'm going to get the nurses in so we can get you ready to deliver." She shook her head and grabbed on the rail.

"Do you want an epidural?" The nurse asked when she came in.

"No. I want my baby natural. No medicines." I shook my head laughing. Even in labor she was showing me how strong she is. Within the next ten minutes a few more nurses and the doctor came in. Once they were all dressed in the scrubs and had on gloves, the doctor lowered the bed and told her its time.

"Each time you feel pain, push." I stood up and started recording on my phone. I could see her roll her eyes.

"AHHHHHHH." She yelled and I stopped recording. One of her eyes became blood shot red. I swear it was bleeding.

"Are you sure you don't want medicine?" The doctor asked and she said no.

I heard some talking outside and looked towards the door and there stood my mom, Dree, Jaime, Robert, my brother and Percy along with his son.

"Not yet y'all."

"Daddy, why aren't you holding her hand?" I hated how smart she was.

"I'm taping it baby and she doesn't want me to touch her right now. It hurts too bad."

167

"I fucking hate you." J said and I busted out laughing.

"Push, Miss Kim. I can see the baby's head."

The doctor opened her lips and I saw the top of his head. I started recording again. She can be mad all she wants but I have Dree being born on video too. All of a sudden, his head popped out. The doctor used some squirt thing to clean his mouth out and he started screaming.

The doctor had her push one more time and his body popped out. Jiao, laid there breathing fast and her eyes were heavy. The nurse took him on the other side of the room, cleaned him up and handed him to me.

"Wait! That's not his son. Give me my baby."

"Yo. Shut the fuck up J. I'm not in the mood and if you wake him up, I'm going to beat your ass." The nurse looked at me and then J.

"Don't mind them. They do this all the time." My mom waved the nurse off and smacked me on the head.

"Why y'all scaring the nurse?"

"Ma, he said he wanted a test, so he doesn't need to bond with him until he gets it."

"Daddy, is this my brother?" I looked up and both J and my mom had their arms folded looking at me. I couldn't do shit but laugh at their petty ass.

"I guess. You have to ask Jiao."

"ANDREEK PURYEAR." J shouted.

"Alright man damn. And stop fucking yelling before you wake my son up. Don't make me say it again." The doctor asked everyone to leave but me so the nurses could clean J up.

"Make sure you clean her pussy good too. I don't want my son around no stinking women." I told the nurse as she helped Jiao in the bathroom. If looks could kill, I would be dead.

"He's hungry Jiao." I told her when she came out the bathroom and he started crying.

"Feed him Dreek."

"Huh?"

"Feed him. I'm tired."

"From what? You didn't do shit."

"I pushed your son out."

"You crazy as hell. He pushed himself out. All you did was lay there."

"Girl, I don't know how you can deal with him. I would never want a baby by.-" Jiao cut her off.

"First of all, don't worry about how I deal with my man. It's your job to assist me in the bathroom and give me pain medication. Not worry about how ignorant he is. We're done here and do me a favor and take your name off as my nurse. I want a new one." I smirked when Jiao let her have it.

"I was just saying."

"But no one asked you to say anything. He is an asshole, a dick and everything else you can think of, but he's mine to worry about. Goodbye." J waved the nurse off and got in the bed.

"Ugh, I'm not your man. Jiao why you ain't let me rap to her, with your blocking ass."

"Not right now Dreek. I can have all the hate I want towards you but no bitch is going to put her two cents in. Now, leave me the fuck alone."

"Yo, who you talking to?"

"My ignorant ass baby father who won't let me relax after his son pushed himself out my pussy." I walked over to the bed.

"Get away from me punk. I'm not in the mood." I leaned in and kissed her lips.

"Thank you for my son."

"Dreek." I know she wanted to apologize again but I'm over it now that he's here.

"I know he's mine J. You needed to hurt the way I did."

"I understand."

"Plus, you were a dead woman if he didn't come out looking like Dree."

"I swear if my son wasn't in your hands, I'd fucking throw this hospital phone at you." I put the towel on my chest and laid him on it to burp.

"Damn, little nigga. You burp loud as hell."

"Dreek, I'm telling you right now, my son is not growing up with your attitude or mouth." I waved her off. Shit, I got my mini me and he's definitely growing up the same as I. A different nurse came in and looked at Jiao, then me.

"Are you crazy girl?" I laughed.

"Excuse me." J sat up. She scrunched her face up.

"Were you drunk when you let this crazy nigga put a baby in you?" J took the covers off and was about to get up. I admit, the way she had my back turned me on.

"Hold up J before you go off."

"Oh shit and she loves you nigga."

"Jiao this is Cameron. Cameron this is my girl Jiao." J almost snapped her neck when I said it.

"Cameron is Jaime's sister."

"Oh ok. I was going to say."

"You must really be in love. No other chick has ever had his back the way you do. They usually let me talk shit and he allows it. How long have you two been together?"

"Girl, knowing him for a day is too damn long."

"Jiao don't make me fuck you up."

"Dreek please. You already know we can get it popping, those other bitches are scared of you but I'm not."

"Ummm. I need your phone number ASAP. I have to take you to meet my family."

172

"Huh?"

"Dreek is like a son to my mom and she always said he'll never meet anyone who will put up with his shit. But damn, he has met his match. I can't wait to call my mom."

"Cameron, go head with that."

"Mmm hmmm. Anyway, Jiao let me take a look at your eye. The doctor wants me to flush it and then put a small gauze on it."

"Do you know why it happened?" I asked and stared at her squirt some solution in her eye. Cameron said because she strained pushing, she most likely popped a few blood vessels. It's going to take some time for it to heal but J will be fine.

"Jiao, do you mind if I take a picture of him to show my mom?"

"What you asking her for? He's my son."

"Go head Cameron. I don't mind and tell your mom I would love to meet her."

"HELL NO."

"Why not Dreek?" Cameron asked with a grin on her face and walked out.

"You don't want me to meet her."

"She's just like my mom and she'll get on your nerves with all the stories about me."

"How long have you known Jaime?"

"All my life and he good peoples. His mom made us promise to keep him safe and so far, so good. Plus, my uncle Owen would kill me if something happened to his son. Him and my uncles ripped me a new asshole when Bash was shot."

"Wait, what?"

"We don't say it a lot because I never want people knowing who my family members are, they prey on shit like that."

"You know they act just alike. I can definitely see the resemblance now that you mention it."

"Jaime's mom can't stand my uncle Owen. She was in love with him at one point from what my mom says, but she will tell you quick, my uncle is a dick."

"It runs in the family."

"It does right but that's their shit. As long as my son knows who his father is, that's all I care about."

174

"Oh, you're his dad now?"

"J, don't play with me."

"What? You said."

"You heard what I said too."

"What's that?" She questioned and wiped my son as she changed him.

"If he didn't look like his sister, you were dead." I shrugged as if it was nothing to kill her. It wasn't, but I know dealing with her death afterwards, would be a bitch.

"I guess." She rolled on her side. I kicked my shoes off and slid in the bed with her. After she cursed me out for causing pain, she made room. The bed is small as hell but we made it work. I took my son from her.

"Wake me up when you leave."

"I'm not leaving." She stared up at me and I leaned down. Once our lips met again, it was like all my love came to surface. She cupped my face and we laid there kissing like two people in love.

"I love you Dreek."

"I know." She smacked my arm.

"I'm playing. I love you too J." She laid on my chest next to our son and fell asleep. This is the family I'm supposed to have and when Dree comes tomorrow, we'll be complete.

Mandy

"Are you sure he said his son's mother?" Samantha asked as she we sat there talking.

I had been avoiding Dreek lately because once I found out it was his daughters' hair I pulled, I knew he would beat my ass. Anyone who knew him, knew his daughter was never to be fucked with. I guess it's why Queenie had black eyes on the regular. I mean the little girl was cursing her ass off as she kicked me. If she acted like that around Queenie, I definitely saw it being a problem.

"Yea, he said if I ever put my hands on his daughter or son's mother again, he'd kill me."

"But you fought Jiao."

"EXACTLY! If he only knew the type of bitch she is, he'd leave her alone."

"What you mean?"

"She isn't the innocent blasian chick people think she is."

"Ok, but so what?"

"So what. Dreek is my man and she's going to learn not to put her hands on me again." I slammed my hand down and went upstairs to take a hot shower. I threw some clothes on and made my way out the door.

"Where you going?" Samantha asked and followed me outside.

"To meet up with someone. You can get your shit and go."

"Excuse me."

"You heard. After you sucked Dreek off, you forgot to get his nut from the corners of your mouth." I don't know why I didn't say anything sooner and beat her ass. I guess I needed someone on my side at the moment.

"Let me explain Mandy."

"Nah, its ok. I know who Dreek is and he probably said some slick shit to you and your dumb ass fell for it."

"Dumb! The only dumb one is you. At least I know what it is and not walking around in denial about a nigga wanting me." I gave her a crazy look.

"You damn right I wanted to try the dick out. Streets talk and I wanted to know what I was missing." She sounded the same way I did when I approached Queenie.

"You're supposed to be my friend." She threw her head back laughing.

"Oh, you mean like how you fucked Brandon and had a baby by him, knowing I had been in love with him since middle school."

"He came after me."

"I know all about you prancing around half naked in front of him at one of the high school parties." I sucked my teeth.

"You see, Brandon may have been fucking you but he told me everything. He even tried to fuck me but I turned him down because I'm not the bitch you are. You even accused Jiao, who at the time was closer to you then me, of sleeping with him. That girl had your back through thick and thin and here you are trying to come up with a plan to get her, in order to get Dreek."

"What the fuck ever?"

179

"Dreek, is not going to allow you to fuck with her, so if I were you, I'd leave well enough alone. Dreek coming back over here, won't be for pussy. Good night." She shoulder checked me and walked to her car.

I jumped in mine and headed to the place I told the bitch to meet up with me at. She and I had unfinished business to discuss.

****

"Why didn't you tell me about Jiao?" I asked Queenie as we sat outside Dunkin Donuts. I sent her a text before getting in the shower telling her we had to meet ASAP.

"Who the fuck cares about her?"

"Ugh, evidently Dreek does. You see my face." She removed her glasses to look at me.

"He did that."

"Yup, because I fought her at the mall and pulled his daughters hair."

"Never fuck with Dree."

"Ugh, I know that now."

"Why were you fighting Jiao anyway?" I started explaining everything and she had her nose turned up.

"She lucky I didn't kick the baby out her stomach."

"What baby?" Queenie looked as if she saw a ghost when I mentioned Jiao's pregnancy.

"Jiao has to be at least eight months or more."

"WHAT? I thought she lost it."

"I don't know what you're talking about. Jiao's stomach is big as hell."

"Fuck. I have to go." She started her car.

"The two of you sitting in the parking lot together can't be a good thing." We both looked up and it was Percy.

"I was leaving."

"Queenie, I've been here watching as you two spoke for the last ten minutes. What did I miss?"

"Nothing. I have to go. Dreek is calling me."

"That's funny. He's looking at you on facetime." Queenie stared in the phone.

"What's up Queenie? Mandy, I see you."

"I'm going home Dreek. Where are you?"

"In the hospital with my son."

"Your son?"

"Yes, my son. Queenie from here on out, don't call me for shit."

"What about our baby?" I laughed so hard when she said that. I knew damn well if she is pregnant, she had no idea who the father is.

"I'll see you when you're in labor. Peace." He hung up and I pulled off.

There's no need for me to stay any longer. Plus, Percy scared me with the way he looked. I wanted to ask when's the last time he heard from Rah Asia but changed my mind. I knew the two of them had been fucking for a minute and she was happy about being pregnant. I wonder if she told him.

"Hello."

"We have to come up with a plan to get rid of the bitch." Queenie said in the phone when I answered and hung up. Finally. Someone who has the same agenda as me.

Queenie

"What the hell is wrong with you?" Marcus asked.

We were lying in the bed after sex and all I could think of were ways to get Jiao. I really shouldn't be thinking about her but the shit has been clouding my mind since Dreek informed me of her giving birth. I knew when she mentioned losing the child, it would push us closer.

However, all it did was make him turn worse towards me. Yea, he fucked me but never stayed the night and only answered my calls when he wanted to fuck. When I questioned him, he snapped and told me to mind my business.

Then Mandy calls me up and confirms she's been sleeping with Dreek for a couple of months. I told the bitch she could fuck him once. She went and made a job out of doing it. I wonder if he fucked us on the same day or what? Dreek, is a piece of shit but his sex game is the shit and as I stated before, no bitch is going to stand next to him, besides me.

I stayed around for too much shit, for him to just leave me in the cold. The beatings, disrespect and other degrading shit he's done to me, puts me in the top spot for the position and I'm getting it by any means necessary.

"I'm good. I have to go."

"Queenie, you've been here for three days and dude hasn't called you. Why are you rushing back?"

"I'm not rushing Marcus but we need to be careful too. You may not care but this baby doesn't deserve to be caught up in the crossfire."

"You better not have told him it's his baby." I didn't say anything and continued getting dressed.

"Queenie, we both know it's my baby and if you even think about not telling me when you deliver, I promise, Dreek will know."

"Marcus, no one ever said this baby is yours." He laughed and walked over to me.

"You didn't have to. We all know Dreek doesn't fuck any bitches without being strapped up. Now, if by some chance you got him to, it was after you were pregnant. I know this because two weeks after we slept together you were already fatigue and showing the signs. And you told me he wouldn't touch you when he first returned from out of town." I thought about what he said and I damn sure run my mouth too much.

"Marcus, we can't tell him the baby is yours but I will call you when I go into labor."

"You a damn fool if you think I'm going to allow him to take care of my first born. What the fuck you on?" I continued to get dressed.

I had to get out of there before he became too angry and did something he'd regret. He's never hit me but when a man is as angry as he is right now, you never know.

"Calm down Marcus. We'll figure it out. There's a few weeks left and honestly, I was thinking about moving away."

"Move for what? Mannnn, I knew I should've never gotten involved with you." I followed him in the other room.

"Don't say that Marcus. You know I love you but we have to be careful. I know you want to watch our baby grow up and so do I. Unfortunately, we can't tell anyone."

"Yea whatever. Call me when you go in labor."

"Babe, I'll be back before then."

"You better be." He kissed me and opened the door for me to leave. For some reason, this dumb bitch Mandy was sitting outside in her car.

"Why is she here?"

"We're going out to eat." I lied but it's the only thing I could come up with.

"Aight. Hit me later." I agreed and made my way to her car. She told me to get in mine and follow her. I didn't ask any questions and did it.

"Lets go." She opened my car door when we pulled up at the local grocery store.

I hit the alarm on my car and went in with her. I'm thinking she wants me to go shopping with her or something but that wasn't the case. She had my big pregnant ass going up and down aisles looking for someone. She ended up leaving me and running to check each one. This bitch is crazy. I decided to go and get me a cart to pick a few things up. I was in the bread aisle when Mandy came and grabbed my arm.

"What the fuck is wrong with you?" I snatched away and stopped when she did.

186

"He doesn't need that Dreek." We stared at Jiao in the store. She was alone and obviously on the phone with my man.

"Bye Dreek. I love you too." Oh hell no. Did this bitch say, I love you too? It means he said it first. What the hell? She hung up and turned around to face both of us.

"Hello ladies." She had a smirk on her face. I noticed her wrap the ponytail up she wore and remove her earrings.

"What you doing all that for?" Mandy asked with her arms folded.

"Oh, because I'm going to beat you ass first and hers second." I didn't get to respond because she started literally beating the breaks off Mandy. Home girl, drug her down the aisle and stomped her out. Me being pregnant did what any woman would do and got the fuck out of there. I'm not scared at all but my baby is more important than a fight. I pressed the unlock button on my key and opened my door.

"Hey Queenie." Why did my dumb ass turn around? I felt a kick to my face and another one to my chest.

"This is for drugging my man in order for him to get your trifling ass pregnant." *How the fuck did she know?* She hit

187

me so hard, I slid down the car and was on the ground. I felt myself going in and out of consciousness. I blocked the kicks and hits as much as I could but she definitely had me at a disadvantage. I can say; not once did I feel any blows to my stomach. I guess she had some sanity about her.

"Stop Jiao. You're going to kill her." I heard a guy say and looked into the eyes of Jaime.

"This is for all the years for fucking with my stepdaughter." I saw her foot coming down on my face and blacked out.

****

"My girl beat that ass, huh?" I heard Dreek say when I opened my eyes. I looked around, and I was in the hospital.

"Why would you let her do that when I'm pregnant with your baby?"

"I didn't allow her to do shit. However, as her man and finding out you drugged me, she took matters into her own hands. I know she made sure you were dealt with for the years of harassing Dree too." I sucked my teeth.

188

"Yo, she fucked you up Queenie. I thought you could fight." Jaime shouted and he found the shit to be hysterical.

"Queenie, I know when you were getting stomped on it was bad, but looking at your face, I see she beat you like a MMA fighter. Damn yo, can you even open your eye?" Jaime and Dreek were cracking jokes like it was funny.

"It's not funny."

"Hell, if it ain't." Jiao said walking in.

"Why aren't you in jail?"

"Because believe it or not, no one called them. You know people are more interested in recording and posting it on social media, than calling the cops. You should log onto Facebook and see how I dragged you and Mandy. It's funny as hell." She stood in front of Dreek and he pulled her close for a kiss.

"Get the fuck out." I shouted and they stopped and stared at me.

"This is how it's going to be Queenie." She came closer.

"Once you have the baby, we're going to test it. If it is indeed his, I'm taking him or her."

189

"No, the fuck you're not."

"Yes, I am." She smirked.

"You see, I know your fucking the help." She whispered in my ear. Dreek and Jaime were laughing at something on the phone. I'm guessing it's the video.

"I don't know what you're talking about." She pulled a phone out and showed me a photo.

"Where did you get that?"

"Oh, your bitch ass friend Mandy. See, she begged for me to stop beating her up, when your punk ass ran out the store. She told me, if I stopped she had something to make my man kill you. At first, I called bullshit until I saw it. This is some good collateral, I must say."

"Fuck you bitch." Out of nowhere, Dreek yanked me by the feet down the bed. My IV popped out and blood started coming out. Some of the monitors came off and the blood pressure cup was tightening around my arm.

"Don't ever come at my girl like that again." He twisted my ankle until it felt as if it snapped. I've never seen him act this way over a chick, not even me.

"Please stop."

"Oh girl, that's nothing. He snapped my shoulder and broke my nose. This is minor." She found the shit funny.

"I can't take your ass nowhere. Get over here Jiao." Jaime said.

"I will literally break every bone in your body if you fuck with her or my daughter in any way, shape or form." The look he gave, had me terrified.

"Is everything ok?" A nurse came in. She smirked at Dreek and Jiao, which let me know they knew one another. I took a better look and noticed she was Jaime's sister Cameron. She hated me too.

"This dumb bitch tried to get up and fell. I think she broke her ankle." Jiao told her.

"Ok, well let's get this fixed. Does this hurt?" Cameron turned my ankle and I screamed out.

"Remember what I said bitch. Oh, and call me when you in labor." Dreek grabbed Jiao's hand and pulled her out the door.

"Damn Queenie. You really on his bad side. I'd hate to be you." She smiled.

"Fuck you."

"That's not nice. Maybe I should call Jiao back."

"Really."

"Really. Now sit your ungrateful ass still so I could put a new IV in your arm." After she finished and cleaned me up of course she talked shit.

"If I were you, I'd leave town. You and I both know if that's not his baby, he's going to kill you for making him think it." She shrugged her shoulders and walked out.

Maybe I should do what she said. Fuck that! Dreek ain't doing shit. I laid on the bed and thought about the ways to get both of them back.

Sommer

"Absolutely not mommy." I said when she tried feeding Raven some French fries from McDonalds. My daughter was almost six months and chunky as hell, thanks to Jiao and Susie. Both of them fed my baby all types of shit and her greedy ass ate it.

"She's hungry Sommer."

"Raven is always hungry. Look at her ma, I have to buy her 2T clothes because of her weight."

"Girl please. Those clothes never fit properly on kids." We both busted out laughing.

Ding, Dong!

The doorbell rung and both of us looked at one another. She shrugged her shoulders and stood up with Raven on her hip. Susie recently moved in this house to get away from my father, who as she says, won't leave her alone. After what he said in the hospital, I understood why he did it, but he also should have never allowed Charlotte to get the power she held over him. I opened the door and tried to slam it back but he stuck his foot in it. Raven damn near jumped out Susie's arms to get to her pathetic ass father.

"I missed you baby girl." He planted tons of kisses on her face. I sucked my teeth and went to walk away and felt him grab my wrist.

"Susie can you keep an eye on her for a few minutes?" He asked and handed her back.

"Ummm sure." Susie knew what the deal was.

"We'll be right outside." He led me out the front door and to his car. He stood in front of it and stared at me.

"I miss you Sommer." I turned my head and rolled my eyes.

"I'm not going to make excuses for what happened but I'm sorry for hurting you. I should have never slept with another woman, regardless if we're a couple or not. You were living with me and we did everything two people in a relationship would."

I let the tears fall. Not because he made me angry but the fact he admitted to his wrong doings. Most men would never and try to deny it. Granted, I had photos but it doesn't matter when it comes to men.

"Sommer, I want us to be a family and I'm standing here right now asking you to be my wife again." He held out a ring bigger then the first one he proposed with.

"Percy, you know I can't."

"Why not?"

"The shit with Kevin."

"I'm not worried about him. He will be handled in due time." He took my hand in his and slid the ring on my finger.

"Percy." He shushed me with his lips.

"I know you need time to forgive me and I'm fine with that. As long as you're my fiancé, I'll wait for you. Take all the time you need. But don't ever keep my daughter away from me again. I don't care how mad you are." I nodded and wiped my face.

"How did you find me?"

"I've always known where you were baby, just like Dreek always knew where Jiao was. Do you really think with the type of men we are, we didn't have eyes on you?"

"Dreek didn't know where J was." He threw his head back laughing.

"In the beginning he didn't, but after she fucked his car up, he knew. Bash told him but made Dreek promise he wouldn't bother her until she was ready."

"That sneaky fuck."

"Sommer, that's his brother. Did the two of you really think he wouldn't say anything?"

"Ugh yea." He found it funny.

"Anyway, once he told me where she was, I knew you were there too. Susie called and told me you were here though." I looked at the door and she was peeking out the window smiling.

"I'm going to kill her." He took my hand in his.

"She and everyone else know we belong together. What I did was fucked up and I apologize. Do you forgive me?"

"I can't make you take all the blame because I allowed it to go on. We weren't having sex and.-"

"I was horny and stupid but don't make any excuses for me. I knew better."

"Yea, but I stayed, which isn't any better."

"It's done and over now. You are my fiancé and I love you to death." He lifted my face.

"Remember the last word." The way he said it made me nervous. Will he really kill me if I didn't want to be with him?

"I'll be home late tonight but my phone is on. If you want to talk, regardless of the time, call me. I'll make sure to answer." I let a small grin come across my face.

"Can I get another kiss before I go?" I never answered because he did it anyway. When we finished, I watched him get in the car and pull off.

"Ma, really." I shut the door and yelled out.

"Sommer, he loves you. I know you missed him."

"Daddy loves you too." She waved me off.

"Ma, I'm serious. He does."

"Well he should have never slept with her." I sat her down and explained everything my dad and Percy told me in the hospital. She was shocked and angry at the same time.

"I'm going to find her. I want some answers."

"I'm coming."

"No, you're not. Raven is here."

"And so is her nanny." I smirked and she sucked her teeth.

"Sommer, I may have to whoop her ass."

"Shit, I'm jumping in. Fuck her." She smiled and gave me a hug. I would never turn my back on Susie. She took care of me when my birth mother threw me away. We hopped in the car and drove straight to the hood to find Miss Charlotte.

****

Susie and I drove around the hood for almost an hour before spotting her. Some dude had her hemmed up against the wall. I had Susie pull up on the side but not too close where she could see us coming. Whoever the guy was, now had his hand around her throat and she was kicking and yelling. I had to laugh because she so damn tough, but here she is screaming bloody murder.

I moved in closer and noticed the person choking her was Robert. *Should I make him stop?* Susie stood next to me and shook her head. Charlotte had tears coming down her face and Robert never removed his hand from her throat. I started to

198

walk away and forget she ever existed but remembered she had a file of some sort that could get Percy and a bunch of others arrested. I wonder if its why he had her up against the wall.

"Robert." He turned to face me and never loosened his grip.

"What you doing on this side of town? And is that your mom? Percy, is going to have a fit."

"Actually, I'm here for her." He turned to Charlotte. Her face was turning blue and the fight in her was dying.

"What you want with this piece of shit?"

"I need to ask her some questions. Can you let her go?"

"Sommer, she shot at Jaime the other day because he wouldn't serve her."

"What? Is he ok?"

"Yea, he got hit on the side but he's good."

"I just need to ask a few questions."

He let go and stood there and said if she ran he was shooting her. He had a few guys come around to block her in. I guess he wasn't playing about killing her. Charlotte fell on the ground holding her neck and gasping for air. I had no remorse and hoped she would hurry up with the theatrics.

"You done." She turned on her knees to stand.

"What do you want?" She had the nerve to snap on me.

"Where is it?" Her laugh was wicked.

"Tell your father to come get it." Susie punched her in the face and kept hitting her. Charlotte tried to fight back but it was no use. I had to tell Robert to get Susie.

"His dick is definitely worth this." She pointed to the split lip and busted nose.

"Where is it Charlotte?"

"What are you going to give me for it?"

"Why would I give you anything? All you gave me was life, nothing more, nothing less."

"HOLD THE FUCK UP! THIS IS YOUR MOTHER?" Robert yelled.

"No, my mother just beat her ass. I only came from her stomach." He didn't question me and let me continue.

"You want something from me, but won't even admit to anyone that I'm your mother." She spit blood out next to my feet.

"I'll tell you what. If you find out where I live, be my guest to invade my space to retrieve it. It will be in a place, you least expect it." The grin on her face was sinister.

"Oh, and if I were you, I'd get to the warehouse your man has and see what the fuck he's hiding from you." She winked and took off.

One of the guys let a few shots off and I saw Charlotte hit the ground but she somehow hopped up and kept going. The guys ran after her and out of nowhere, a car pulled up and she jumped in it. Gunfire erupted on the street and Robert jumped on me and snatched Susie on the ground. The shit sounded as if we were in a movie.

Once it stopped, I heard a car coming down the street with the music blasting. It stopped in front of me as Robert and one of the other guys helped us up off the ground.

"GET IN THE FUCKING CAR AND I DARE YOU TO SAY SOMETHING." Percy barked and I looked at Susie, who appeared to be nervous for me. Him and my dad always told me not to come on this side and I see why.

"Thanks for keeping them safe." Percy told Robert.

"You already know." They shook hands and Percy had all of them disperse before any cops showed up.

"Well today was interesting."

"What were you doing here Sommer?" I tried to explain but he cut me off and answered his phone. He spoke for a few minutes, to who I'm assuming was Dreek and hung up.

"Ever since we found out who Charlotte was, she's become a pain in the ass. Jaime told her she couldn't cop drugs from anyone, anymore and she shot him. It wasn't bad but enough for us to question what she even had a gun for. This is the second time she got away. Whoever she's working with must stay around in case shit pops off. We don't know who it is before you ask and just so you know, she's a dead woman walking."

"Wait! We have to find out where she lives."

"We know where she stays."

"Take me there. She claims to have the file there." I never told him what she said about going to the warehouse because I'm going to pop up when he least expects it.

Percy

The entire drive to get where Sommer was, my heart was racing. I could hear the gunshots as I got closer and prayed she wasn't hit. I admit when Robert text me she was there, I was pissed but I knew she wanted answers from Charlotte. I should have taken Sommer to talk with her sooner. Unfortunately, she shot Jaime and with the other shit I had going on at the warehouse, a nigga was stressed and forgot.

I parked down the street from the house we knew to be Charlotte's and sat there waiting. We could go barging in but that would be stupid when we had no idea if she were here or who she had inside. I sent Robert a test to come here with a few guys. I needed to make sure when we went in, no one would catch us slipping.

After sitting in silence for an hour and seeing no movement or lights on, Sommer and I stepped out the car and made our way down the street. It wasn't real dark out yet, however, we still didn't take chances on not being seen.

I kicked the door open and we went in leaving it cracked. We both started searching and couldn't find shit. I asked Sommer what exactly Charlotte said and something must've clicked because she ran in the room and snatched a photo of her father up and turned it around. I'm wondering why she even had a photo of him at all.

She peeled the back of the frame off and sure enough there was a piece of paper. Sommer handed it to me and I opened it up. It was her birth certificate and a sticky note with directions to go in her bathroom, look under the cabinet and push the wall back. We ran in there and what do you know? There was a small safe and a bunch of photos. I took everything out and used the flashlight on my phone to make sure we didn't leave anything behind.

"Percy, let's put everything back so she thinks we never came." I looked at her.

"She's going to know because of the door."

"Yea, but can't you get someone here to fix it really quick."

"I guess. The only thing broke is the wood on the side. Let me make a call." I set it up and waited twenty minutes for the guy to arrive. In the meantime, I had the guys come in and help us clean. Sommer and I really fucked the house up, searching for the shit.

When the guy finished and the house seemed to be in order, we left and drove to my house. I opened the door and she came in and went straight to the kitchen. I saw her grab a small knife out the utensil drawer and try to open the safe. I took it from her and stepped out on the patio. I sat the safe on the ground, pulled my gun out and shot at the lock. After two times, it appeared to be broke. She ran over and opened it.

"Oh my God Percy. Look at this." She handed me papers. They were discoveries on some of my soldiers who are doing hard time for distributions, selling guns, and a bunch of other shit. The most bizarre thing of it all, is she had another birth certificate with a guy's name on it.

"No. It can't be." She stood up and paced the backyard.

"Baby calm down."

"Percy, there's no way my father had another kid and never told me."

"He didn't sign the birth certificate, which means he probably doesn't know."

"It's his son." We heard and turned around to see Susie standing there with tears coming down her face. I knew she was on her way over with Raven, who was asleep on her shoulder.

"Are you sure?"

"I'm asking you. Does your father have another kid?" Sommer ran over and hugged her.

"I don't know ma. If he did, it was before you because this guy is a year older than me. But if he's my brother, how was Charlotte able to keep him a secret? Was she on drugs with him too? It doesn't make sense?" All of a sudden, Sommer went into a shaking fit and it was worse than I've ever seen.

"Call 911. She's having a seizure." Susie yelled out. Her eyes were rolling and foam spilled from her mouth. Susie laid Raven on one of the lawn chairs and ran to Sommer.

"Hurry up." I watched Susie lay Sommer on her side as I gave my address to the people.

****

"Hey babe." Sommer whispered as I sat it the chair looking through the paperwork we found.

After the ambulance picked her up, I called Dreek and asked if him and Jiao could watch Raven while I went to the hospital. He came to pick her up because Jiao was still in pain from delivering. I threw everything in a small bag and drove to be with Sommer.

"How you feeling?" I asked and placed the papers on the chair.

"Ok. Where's Raven?"

"Jiao has her." She nodded and asked me to help her get out the bed to use the bathroom.

"Sommer, you can't stress yourself out the way you did. Baby, you had a seizure and it was bad."

208

"I'm sorry Percy. When I get upset, I can't help it."

"I'm going to try and make sure you don't stress anymore." I kissed her lips and she moved over in the bed for me.

"Do you think we should tell him he's my brother? But if he's my brother, then who's his dad?"

"You have to ask your father."

"I'm his father." Her dad stepped in the room.

"Daddy." She reached out and he came to hug her.

"What's going on?" He sat down and started explaining himself. Susie came in a few minutes later holding my daughter.

"I met your mother about twenty-eight years ago at a bar. She and I had sex on the first night, and a few times after. We were young and none of us thought of using protection. Anyway, it was if she disappeared and I didn't see her again until I saw her pushing a little boy in the baby stroller. Of course, she denied he was mine and that she was putting him up for adoption. I never thought to look into it and went about my business."

"He didn't look like you." Sommer asked.

"I think the baby was a few months old. I never paid attention. Long story short, we hooked up again and I had no idea she was on drugs until you were almost born." I gave him the side-eye.

"Believe it or not, Charlotte hid it very well. By that time, she and I were barely speaking and I met Susie. Once she gave birth, I banned her from coming to the hospital until she was clean. At no point did she even make an attempt to see you, which let me know, she had no idea about the ban and the drugs were more important. I stayed at the hospital damn near all day and night. When you came home, I didn't have to ask Susie anything. She jumped right in as your mom and you know everything from there." She nodded.

"I've tried plenty of times to get her to see you and she always declined. Did I mess around and sleep with her a few times? Yes. But never without protection nor did I spend an entire weekend with her. It happened two years ago when Susie kept asking me to have kids. I was upset and tired of hearing about it, went out, ran into her and carried on a few times."

"But she said you gave her two kids." Susie stood there crying as he spoke.

"Charlotte said those things to hurt Susie. Everyone knows Susie is your mom and how much they love her. It's not a secret she doesn't have children of her own, so Charlotte shouted it out, in order to break us up, which she did."

"But why does she want you away from Susie?"

"Because she feels like Susie is the reason we could never be together again and it's the truth. I would never leave my wife for any woman. Yes, I messed up years ago, but not one day goes by where I think of another woman." He stood up in front of Susie.

"You can hate me for cheating on you years ago, but I am still very much in love with you. Your side of the bed has been waiting to feel you in it since you left." He kissed her and she didn't stop him.

"But how do you know he's your son?" Sommer was asking him a million questions but I get it. He stopped kissing his wife to answer.

"I did some research when she shouted the other two false pregnancies out. She did give the kid up for adoption. When I received the documents, it stated the father was unknown. I noticed his blood type and it's the same as mine and yours. I can say he's mine, but I would rather get a test done first."

"How are we going to do that?"

"He's on his way now."

"Hey Sommer." Dreek said. She looked behind him for J but he told her she didn't want to leave the baby.

"Hey yall."

"Who's going to tell him?" None of us said a word. I guess I'll do it.

"Yo, Robert. We have to talk to you."

"What's up? He glanced around the room at all of us.

"Robert have you spoken with your parents about any relatives?" Sommer's dad asked and we waited to hear his response.

"Actually, we recently had this conversation a few days ago.

"What did they tell you?"

"Oh, that I'm adopted and the woman who birthed me was and still is a crackhead."

"Yo, why y'all asking him mad questions?" Dreek asked looking as confused as Robert.

"It looks like they just found out Sommer is my sister, the same way I did." Sommer's mouth dropped open and so did everyone else's.

"Before you ask, I was going to talk to you about it but the shit happened with Charlotte and now you're here. So, are you supposed to be my pops?"

"But you were about to kill Charlotte." Sommer said and didn't let her father answer.

"And?"

"And, you're not the least bit concerned on why she gave you up and never revealed who your dad was?"

"Not at all. My parents are all I know. Her name on the birth certificate don't mean shit. Plus, she shot Jaime and everyone knows him, Percy and Dreek are like my brothers. Now that I know for sure you're my sister, you'll be even more protected than what my brother in law already has in place."

"Um, this went a lot better than I expected." Her father said.

"Listen Robert, once I saw the documents, I noticed all three of us have the same blood type. I feel you're mine but I want to take a test to be sure."

"I'm cool with that." He shrugged and Sommer's dad walked out the room. Him and a nurse came in asking who the person was she had to test. It's crazy how her pops still had pull to get shit done.

After the two of them stepped out and went downstairs, Susie and Dreek left too. He had to go address some shit with his ex and Susie said she needed to be alone to deal with all of this. She handed me Raven and promised to call Sommer tomorrow.

"You ok babe?" I asked and watched her change my daughter.

"Yea. It's crazy to find out after all these years but then again, I guess you can't expect much from her."

"You're right but we still have to find out what's on this disk and who she's working with."

"What were in the papers?" I told her and she shook her head.

"That is one wicked woman. I'm glad she left me at the hospital. I wouldn't have wanted to grow up with her."

"Good thing you didn't." I laid in the bed and fell asleep next to them until the doctor woke us up and said she could go home. We had to handle this shit with Charlotte and soon. I can't have my wife having all these shaking attacks over her bullshit.

Dreek

After leaving the hospital and finding out Robert and Sommer are related, I made a stop by Queenie's. Not on no sex type shit. But to find out how the pregnancy is going. Half of me believes it could be my kid and the other, I'm not sure about. Had J not talked me into finding out for sure, I wouldn't have come.

I wanted to kill her when dude came back and told me the glass had some shit in it. The drug enhanced the liquor and well, we all know what happened then. Jiao wanted to murder Queenie but then again, because we didn't know if the kid is mine or not, I asked her not to. Unfortunately, she is very pigheaded and whooped her ass. She still made plans to murk her after the baby came.

"Dreek. What are you doing here?" Queenie asked like she was surprised.

"I came to find out when your due date is."

"Another week. You coming in."

"Nah, I'm good."

217

"Really Dreek. We've been together way too long for you to act this way towards me."

"Let me say this to you." I stepped off the porch and had her follow me to my car." I handed her over the paper saying she spiked my drink. She had the nerve to ball the paper up and throw it across the parking lot.

"All the years we've been together, not once did I think you were capable of doing some crazy shit like this to me."

"Dreek. I.-"

"I don't want to hear why you did it. If you weren't pregnant right now with the possibility of the kid being mine, I would've already shot you between the eyes."

"Why are you treating me this way?" I scoffed up a laugh.

"Queenie, over the last year and a half, I've allowed you to get away with a lot of shit; especially when it came to my daughter." That's how long Dree's mom has been gone and before that, Dree never came over if Queenie was around. Evidently, Dree hated her long before I knew and her mom didn't play that shit.

"You know your daughter and I have a love/ hate relationship."

"Bitch are you crazy? Dree hates you and it's too bad I didn't take the steps of removing you from my life sooner. I figured Dree was acting out due to her mom passing away and I kept you around as a mother figure. However, Dree may have fucked with you a lot but she is still a child. Now that I think about it, did you ever try and comfort or even talk to her. I know it's not your job but look at my girl." She sucked her teeth at the mention of Jiao.

"She didn't know Dree at all the day in the mall and they instantly formed a bond. The connection was strong from the very beginning and I admit, it's what made me start falling for her."

"Why did you lie when I asked if you loved her?"

"In the beginning, I didn't. I wasn't sure of the feelings I felt around her, nor did I want to start anything with a chick I had to beat up. Do you remember how bad I whooped my girls' ass?" She had the nerve to smirk.

"Not once did she back down from me and anytime we were around one another, she made sure I respected her or we would go at it again. That's when I realized she was the one for me. No woman dared to challenge me like her."

"Dreek, I was scared."

"And she wasn't." I moved closer to her.

"You think I wanted a weak woman by my side who couldn't even make my daughter like her? Or one, who allowed me to beat on her and still let me fuck? You didn't care what I did to you, as long as you could claim me. The sad part is, you went as far as allowing Mandy to fuck me so she wouldn't tell some secret."

"I don't know what you're talking about." She folded her arms across her chest.

"I don't know what Mandy spoke of either but if you're willing to let your so-called man fuck other chicks to keep a secret, your self-esteem is extremely low and you need to figure out how to fix it." I asked Mandy after the first few times we had sex why she finally approached me and she clearly stated, *"Queenie told me to try my luck."* I knew then something was up because when Mandy tried previously, Queenie almost beat her ass in the club.

"I stayed with you Dreek because I thought one day you'd wake up and see I'm the woman for you." I shook my head. This chick is in denial.

"I could never love a woman who doesn't love herself Queenie and that's some real shit."

"What you trying to say?"

"I've said more than enough for you to catch on."

"Dreek, I love you."

"You can continue saying it until you're blue in the face. It won't make me want you."

"But why?"

"Because I fucked up and put you before my daughter and I have to live with that for the rest of my life."

"No you didn't."

"Every time you fucked with her on the sneak tip, every time you argued with her like an adult and each time I beat your ass and still fucked with you, put you ahead of her. After the first time, I should've left you alone but trying to give her a mother, made me keep you. It's not an excuse and I will have to make this shit up to Dree, which I don't have a problem doing because I was wrong."

"But Dreek, you know Dree was doing mad shit to me."

"Dree has her flaws like all kids but you're a grown woman and know better. I'm good on you Queenie."

"Don't leave Dreek. I want us to be friends for the baby." I opened the door to my car, sat down and rolled my window down.

"You heard my girl when she said if that's my baby, she's taking it."

"Over my dead body will she get my child."

"I think we both know, me or Jiao won't have a problem accommodating that request for you." I hit her with the peace sign and bounced.

****

"Stop saying that shit J." I told her when we got in the car.

I had just gone to the doctor with her for the six-week checkup shit. The doctor asked if she ever had any dislocations before and her crazy ass said yes and told her what happened. She said it the day she beat Queenie up and I broke that dumb bitch's ankle too. I wasn't going to say anything but she mentioned it again.

"Saying what?" I watched her put on the seatbelt.

"About me snapping your arm and shit."

"You did."

I don't regret beating her ass the night we first met because I felt like she deserved it. But ever since I fell in love, I would never put my hands on her again. Well, I'm going to try not to. As we all know, my anger and temper turns me into another person. The thought hurting her now, is not something I see myself doing.

"Ok, but it's old and I don't.-" I swerved a little.

"Stop J. Fuck yo." I had to let the moan out. She had pulled my sweats and boxers down a little, while I was in mid conversation and swallowed me.

"Shit. I need to pull over."

"Don't stop or people will know." She lifted her head to say.

"J, there's no way. Oh shitttttt." I felt my nut coming to the top and had no choice but to stop or we would've been dead. This is the first time I felt any type of pleasure since she had my son. I never asked her to be my girl but the night she had my son, no words had to be said for us to know what it was.

"Fuck baby. Got damn." Her hand stroked my shaft fast and next thing I know, she swallowed every drop. I yanked her up by the hair and stared.

"You the shit J."

"I know." She climbed over in the driver side.

"Not at all J. Get up."

"Dreekkkkkkkk, I wanna do it in the car." She whined and I laughed.

"J, you had a baby, which means your pussy is back to being virgin tight." I squeezed her ass and she moaned in my ear.

"I need more space to bust that ass open." She punched me in the arm and sat in the passenger seat pouting.

"J, I got you after the first time. How you acting spoiled already? I swear, you and Dree got me fucked up."

"I'm spoiled."

"Hell yea you are." She rolled her eyes.

"You live in a brand-new house, push a 2018 Cayenne, have tons of shoes, purses, and clothes you had to have, in the closet. Plus, you get to wake up and go to bed with me every night."

"Oh, the joy."

"Oh yea. How about I drop your ass off and wake up to some other chick who's going to appreciate me?"

"I wish the fuck you would. I'll burn you, the bitch and any other living creature in the house down. And that's after I beat her ass and get my few hits in on you."

225

I laughed hard as hell. She was dead serious but I loved it. Jiao definitely loved me with all my flaws. No woman could ever get me the way she has and that's wrapped around her finger.

"What would you say if I allowed a nigga to entertain me on the phone?" She said as we pulled up to the house.

"Try me and see."

"Ok, well this guy I met when we weren't talking is still texting and wants to take me out."

"Word."

"Word."

"Tell him we'll meet him at the movies and he can pay for everything. I may even let him watch me finger pop you in the back."

"I fucking hate you." She walked ahead of me and I picked her up from behind.

"Get off me loser."

"I bet after you get this dick, I won't be a loser anymore."

"Goodnight Dreek." She tried to close the door.

226

"What you doing?" I pushed the door opened.

"Oh, you said you were going to wake up with someone else. I'm going to allow you to leave and when you smell smoke, don't jump up."

"You got that. I'm out." Just like I thought. Her crazy ass came running behind me and jumped on my back.

"Jiao, you're about to start and the kids are home." She was sucking on my neck.

"I want you so bad baby." I made her get off, only to lift her in front of me, wrap her legs around my waist and pull my sweats and boxers down in the front.

"How bad you want it J?" She had on a pair of jeans and slid them past her ass, along with her panties. It was uncomfortable as hell but baby girl got whatever she wanted from me.

"Fuck Dreek. Real bad." I let the head touch the top of her pussy and she was soaking wet.

"I can't tell." I kept playing around her entrance and she was squirming to make me put him in.

"Oh shitttt Dreek." She put her tongue in my mouth to stifle the scream I know she wanted to let out. The further I pushed in, the more I felt her nails digging in my back. It felt like the first time we were together.

"Damn J. You about to make me cum already." She was drenched and her walls were squeezing the shit out of me.

"Not yet Dreek. It feels so good. Ssssssss." She went from kissing me to sucking on my neck.

"I'm cumming Dreek. Fuck yea." I felt her juices running down my leg, lifted her off and watched her stroke my dick as I came. I'm telling you, J had my mind gone and if anyone dared to fuck with her, they were dead on sight.

"I love you so much Dreek." I pulled my pants up, helped her with her jeans and lifted her face.

"What's wrong?"

"Nothing. I know you've never been in love and you're still trying to wrap your head around it but I want you to know, that you are the only man I love and I would do anything for you and the kids, remember that." I'm not sure how to take what she said but I appreciated the fuck out of her for always telling me how she felt.

"J, you know I'm a man of little words but know you are the only woman I have and will probably ever love. I guess you can say, I'm in love with you too."

"Huh?"

"What I mean is, I've never felt the way I do when we're together. I told you before, I love waking up and going to bed with you. I love the way you love my kids and my family. The constant I love you's, from you make it all worth it, because I know I'm not in this alone. One day you may be my wife but until then, you'll be right here by my side." I wrapped my arms around her waist and held her in front of me.

"Why are you crying?"

"Because Dreek, that's probably the nicest thing you've ever said to me."

"Just know I may not say how I feel but I promise to show you. If you ever need to hear me say it, tell me. I'm new to this and I don't know how many times a woman should hear it." She started laughing.

"I mean it Jiao. I can honestly say you are more than enough woman for me and I no longer have to rent my dick out."

"You always know how to mess up a mood." She went to walk in the house.

"I'm learning to control my mouth but it's hard."

"Well don't control it when it comes to pleasing me." She turned around with a big grin on her face.

"Get your nasty ass in the house. You already walking funny but you still want your pussy ate."

"That's because I have the pussy eating King as my man."

"And don't you forget it. Now get the kids ready, I'm taking them to my mom's like you asked. I'm tearing my pussy up." She walked up the steps slowly and I shook my head laughing. The things women do for men. Her pussy is probably swollen and sore, yet, she's still willing to please me. It's the little shit I love when it comes to her and that's why she has a secured position in my life.

Jiao

"Damn J." Dreek moaned out and wrapped his hands around my hair as I bobbed up and down his shaft with my mouth. I stopped and let a little spit drop on it and continued.

"Shitttttt." I let my tongue slide down and began sucking on each one of his balls gently. My tongue flickered under them and he moaned a little louder.

"I'm about to cum J. Get up." I always laugh when he tried to make me stop. His ass is already in love so he may as well stop asking. He told me the reason he never wanted me to swallow and in my opinion, it's a dumb reason. Shit, I cum in his mouth all the time.

"Yea baby. Mmmmm, you taste so good." I made sure to moan and suck as he came. It turned me on even more.

"Sit on my face J." I never objected when he wanted certain things in the bedroom. As of right now, he's my first and last unless he fucks up.

"Dreeek, you don't even give me time to. Fuckkkkkk." I came right away. My body succumbed to him every time his tongue touched my pearl. It's like she waited for him to suck on her.

"Keep cumming for me J. Yea, like that." He stuck his finger inside, found my g-spot and I came so hard, he had to catch me from falling off the side of the bed.

"You think you're the only one who could make someone tap out?" He asked and sat me on top of him.

"Noooooo."

"Don't cover your face. I love seeing your expressions." I moved slowly to bond with his size as always and took over.

"Damn J. I taught you very well. Shit woman." I heard him say and clenched my muscles together.

"Yea. Like that." He squeezed my ass cheeks and sat up to kiss me.

"I love you Andreek Puryear."

"I love you too Jiao Kim. Mmmm shit, I'm about to cum and I want you to cum with me." He rubbed my clit and in seconds we came together. He wrapped his arms around my back as I laid my head in the crook of his neck.

"You have some good pussy baby."

"You made it that way."

"You're right." I mushed him on the side of the head and went to shower.

He was right behind me and slid in the shower and inside me. Once the doctor told us we could have sex again, we've been at it like animals in heat. We could have had sex two weeks after having my son but I refused to get pregnant right away. I wanted the birth control to kick in and he agreed. Both of us wanted more kids but right now things are too hectic.

"What you doing today?" He asked and dried me off.

"My dad wants to see me." I shrugged when he stared at me.

"I know your dad from somewhere J. I can't figure out where but I do."

"It's probably because your brother was messing with my mom. Everyone knows they were married."

"I figured out where I knew your mom from, once Bash told me but your dad is a different story." I put my bra on and stared at him sit there in deep thought.

"J, I'm about to as you something and I don't want you to get upset."

"What?"

"Do you think your dad had something to do with your moms' death?

"I thought about it already Dreek and honestly, I don't know. I wish I could say no but the way he's been acting, has me looking at him funny."

"When did you start thinking it?"

"The day of the funeral. He barely shed any tears and at the repass, he allowed some woman to feel all over him. I handled it but the woman never should have felt comfortable doing it. What really made me suspicious is when I went to her grave and he didn't come. I figured he had company so I excused it. I came in the house and he had a non chalant attitude and even told me he doubts my mother missed him visiting."

"Damn J." I stood in front of him on the bed and kneeled down in front of him.

"Dreek, if he is indeed the man who murdered my mother, I promise you, I'm going to kill him and I put that on my life." He cupped my face with his hands.

"Jiao, I know you're able to handle yourself but if you find out he did it, I swear he's a dead man. The person who killed her, is responsible for you almost killing my brother and for that alone, he has to die. My son lost his grandmother way too soon and my girl hasn't been right since." I started crying thinking about how happy my mom would be meeting him and my son. She would get a kick out of how we met though.

"Dreek, I would never ask you to take on my battles."

"It's my responsibility to do it without you asking." He lifted my head.

"Stop crying J. You have to be strong to deal with the possibility of it being him."

"I know but what if it is? Could I kill him?"

"And that's the exact reason why I would. No one ever wants to kill their parent and I know for a fact you would hesitate, the same way I would if my mom did some foul shit. I would want to know why and wonder if I could ever forgive her. J, you are tough as nails but let me handle this. If you want to watch, I'll let you. If you don't, I'm ok with that too. But something as serious as this, if it is the case, will be hard on you, or any child."

"Dreek."

"Just know I got you J and I won't let anyone hurt you again, including myself."

"How in the hell did I get your mean and aggressive ass to fall in love with me?"

"That pussy and head game did it." I smiled. He gave me a serious look and spoke some real shit.

"You loved and protected my daughter from the first day you met her and I will always love you or it. Your strength and willingness to teach me how to love, is what got me too. You saw past everything and took a chance. You made me see what I was missing not having a strong woman by my side and I hope you know, you're stuck."

"I want to be stuck but only with you." He stood up with me and threw me over his shoulder.

"Put me down." I yelled as he took me out the bedroom.

"If I do, I may have to dick you down. I mean all this sentimental shit got me horny."

"Ugh, you get on my nerves." He put me down in front of my son's door and ran in before me to get him. We fought so much on who would hold him and today he beat me to him. I left him in there and went to get Dree up.

"Get up Dree. I'm taking you to nana's."

"I don't want to go over there."

"Why not?" I heard Dreek ask behind me with lil Dreek on his chest. Dree sat up.

"Because Nana never lets me hold my brother. Then she shows him off at the stores but I can't push him in the stroller either." She was big mad over her nana. Dreek and I both busted out laughing. I sat next to her.

"Dree, you have to remember, you live here and hold him all the time. Nana sees him once or twice a week, so of course she wants to hold him more. If you hurry up and get yourself together, you can hold him until we leave and I'll stay over for a little so you can show nana you're a big girl when it comes to your brother. Maybe, she'll let you then." She gave me a hug and jumped out the bed. I heard the shower go on in her bathroom and Dreek and I stepped out to give her privacy.

"That is exactly why you have the wife position. See, I would've told her ass to get over it and she'll hold him when he's here."

"It's because you're a man and don't know how to speak to girls."

"Whatever. If you ask me, she's being a brat like her stepmother."

"Yea well, this stepmother earned her spoiled position and one reason is because of who you're holding."

"Yo, don't throw my son in your bullshit reasons. Now if you said your pussy was the reason or the way you suck my balls, then you can get that."

"Get away from me Dreek. We promised never to lay hands on each other again but you make it so hard."

"Don't think I haven't thought about dragging your ass either. Now leave me and my son alone." I shook my head laughing at him. I hate to say it but he and I are perfect for one another; regardless of our past. I don't see myself with anyone else and I pray he feels the same. I would hate for my son to grow up fatherless because I damn sure would kill him if he ever cheated.

****

"Long time no see daughter." My dad sarcastically said when I stepped in the house.

"Hello dad."

I picked up the mail off the counter and rummaged through it. Nothing was of importance except one from an unknown address and it had my dad's name on it. I doubt he even knew it was there because it was so much mail, I wouldn't have either. Since his back was turned, I slid the envelope in my purse and made my way up the stairs. I have no idea what made me go up there.

I opened the door and glanced around the room my mom used as her closet. She was like me when it came to shopping. There were so many purses, shoes and a bunch of clothes with tags still on them. I sat on the small loveseat she had and let my head rest on the back of it. My dad came in and sat next to me.

"Its time dad." I spoke of getting rid of my mom's things. It's been over four years now and he hadn't touched a thing.

"I know sweetie. Take what you want and I'll have someone from the goodwill pick the rest up." He left me sitting there.

"Hey. You good." Dreek asked when he answered. He was out with Percy and I told him I'd call to let him know I was ok.

"Yea. I miss you."

"Ah shit J. The dickdown from this morning got you missing me."

CLICK! I hung up on his crazy ass. My phone rung back.

"I told you about hanging up on me. J don't make me come over there."

"Maybe I want you to come."

"You should've just said it. I'll be there in a few." He hung up on me.

I had every intention of calling him back until I felt something in one of the shoeboxes. My mom wore a lot of heels and I know the box isn't this heavy. I removed the lid and there were no shoes but quite a few notebooks. I opened one and it was dated.

July 1, 2013,

He brought his sexy ass back in the shop again and I couldn't help but have butterflies like I did whenever he came. Here I am a married woman and having sexual thoughts about being with another man. He's younger than me for sure but God is he sexy. The way he walks, talks and smiles. I love my husband but this man does something to me each time he comes in.

July 2, 2013

Today the guy came in again and this time we spoke. I found out his name is Bash and like I thought, he is younger. He and I talked for a good two hours in the store. If my husband found out I entertained another man, he'd probably

beat my ass. Lord knows after the last beating, I thought my

daughter would find out. How does a man beat on a woman

who finds out he's cheating on her? It isn't my fault he got

caught, but in due time I'm leaving him. This woman is the

sixth one in the last few years and I'm over it.

"J, you in here?" I heard Dreek's voice and wiped my

eyes. I hid the book in case my dad walked him up.

"What's wrong?" He came over to me and I hugged

him tight.

"J, you're shaking. Tell me what's wrong." He waited

for me to calm down and moved me back. I shut the door,

locked it and put some music on my phone. I handed him the

book and sat next to him.

"Damn J. I'm sorry you found out this way."

"Why didn't she say anything about the beatings?"

"J, Bash told me your mom wanted you to keep the

perfect image of her and your father. She probably didn't want

you to worry."

"Dreek, I'm ready to go." I grabbed the books and headed for the door.

"Jiao, you have to put them in a bag or something. He's not going to be ok with you walking out with them."

"I don't care what he wants."

"J, control your emotions baby. You're upset but you can't allow him to think anything or you'll never find out the truth."

"Dreek, he was beating and cheating on her."

"I know J but be smart about how you approach the situation. Come on, let's put some stuff in a bag. What do you want to take? Shit, I hope it ain't a lot because you have mad shit at the house." He glanced around the room and said now he saw why I had so much.

"Come here Jiao." He stood by a wall in the closet and stared at me.

"What?" I had no idea what I'm looking at. He pushed the wall and a small piece of it opened. I looked up at him and he shrugged his shoulders. I watched him turn the flashlight on and look inside.

"Ummm, you need to see this." He stepped out and let me go in.

I covered my mouth. There were stacks of money inside. I'm not talking a few here and there, I'm talking about money stacked to the ceiling. Where did she get it from and how did my father not find it? He picked up his phone and made a call right away.

"Yo. Do me a favor. Have someone contact the police department and make a bomb threat to Jiao's father Chinese restaurant. I need her dad out of this house. Also, I need you, Robert and Jaime to come here ASAP. Make sure you have someone keep an eye on her father at the restaurant and give us a heads up when he leaves. I grabbed the envelope taped to the wall.

Jiao if you're reading this, it means I am no longer here. I know you're wondering where all this money came from and it's not what you think. I didn't rob a bank or steal from anyone. My mother, your grandmother died when you were a baby and left me an insurance policy of a hundred thousand dollars. I put it in the bank under your name, however, your father got wind of it and tried to take it. Yes, he did and don't let him tell you different. He was in debt to some guy and tried to use your money to pay him off but I wouldn't let him. I tried asking what was going on but he never told me.

"Jiao something happened at one of the restaurants. Lock up when you leave." My father yelled through the door.

"Ok." I never opened the door and went back to reading the letter.

Anyway, I removed it from the bank and kept it hidden here. I pray you find this before him. Over the years I've added to it. Any money your dad gave me, always went in the bank and I would withdraw from it occasionally so he wouldn't think anything of it.

Jiao, your father isn't who he claims to be at all and you should stay clear of him. I love you so much and I know you're probably wondering why I never told you. Honey, parents don't want to put their problems on their kids. When you have some of your own, you'll see.

Jiao when you find a man, make sure he respects you.
Don't allow him to walk over you or treat you like shit. You'll
know he's the right man because he'll try you any chance he
gets. You are very strong willed and it will take a strong-
minded man to deal with you and your attitude. I'm going to
miss my grandbabies grow up, the birthdays, your wedding,
and anything else but know I'm watching over all of you.

P.S. If you happen to see the guy Bash, tell him I loved
him and should've listened when he told me to run away with
him all those times. I'm sorry for not getting out sooner but I
couldn't leave you. I love you Jiao and stay safe.

"I hate him." I stepped out the room and handed Dreek
the letter. I went downstairs, found a hammer and was about to
destroy the house.

"It's not worth it J. I promise, I got you baby." He held
me and let me cry in his arms.

"Yo, what happened to her." Percy asked when they
came rushing through the door.

"I'll tell you later. Look." He wiped my face with his
shirt.

"Upstairs is a wall inside the closet. I need y'all to take everything out of it and bring it to the house. There's a box with some books in it, make sure it's the first thing you bring out." They all nodded.

"Did y'all come together?"

"Robert and Jaime did. What's up?"

"Can one of you drive her truck? I don't want her to return here for any reason."

"You sure she good?"

"She will be." He lifted me up, carried me out to his car and placed me inside. I laid my head on his shoulder when he sat down. His hand intertwined with mine as we drove home.

"Ma, can you keep the kids tonight?" She must've asked what happened and he told her he would tell her later.

"Let me talk to her." He handed me the phone.

"Ma, you know I love you right?"

"What's wrong Jiao? Is everything ok?"

"Yes, it has to do with my father but we'll fill you in later. I wanted to talk to you because I need you to let my daughter hold her brother." She sucked her teeth. I felt Dreek squeeze my hand when I said daughter instead of step. I wasn't trying to take the place of her mom but step seemed informal.

"Dree is fine."

"Ma, please do this."

"Whatever. He's sleeping with me." I laughed and hung the phone up.

She can be so petty at times. I looked up at Dreek who was now on the phone with Bash and smiled. My mom was right about meeting a guy who could handle me and that guy, is Andreek Puryear.

Bash

"I need you to come over real quick." Dreek spoke in the phone when I answered.

"You good." I asked.

"Yea. Jiao asked me to have you come. She has something to give you."

"Aight. I'm holding my nephew right now but I'll be over."

"Oh shit. I didn't know you were at moms. I could have had her put you on the phone."

"I just got here. I'm on my way." I hung up and felt someone staring at me.

"Is Jiao ok?" Dree asked with a sad look on her face.

"She's fine. Why would you ask that?"

"Because nana said we're sleeping over and Jiao always tells me if we are or not. She didn't call me." I sent Dreek a text and told him to have Jiao call my niece. I could see how attached she was and understood why she would feel that way. A few minutes later my mom's phone rang and she called Dree in the room.

"Hey babe. I get off at seven. Are we still on for dinner?" Cameron asked. Yes, it's the same Cameron who is related to Jaime. Before anyone thinks it, they have different fathers so we're not related.

The day Jiao gave birth to my nephew, we ran into each other; literally. I knocked folders out her hand by accident from not paying attention. She started cursing me out until she realized who I was. The two of us ended up exchanging numbers and have been talking and texting nonstop.

Cameron wasn't your average hood chick. She had a good ass job as a RN and she was the supervisor on her floor. She was very pretty and I would always tell her she resembled Aaliyah. She hated it and not because Aaliyah is ugly but she wanted her own look. Cameron didn't want anyone dating her or even sexing her thinking of Aaliyah. I always laugh when she says it because who in the hell would do some shit like that?

"Yea. I'm on my way to my brother's house. Jiao has something she wants to give me."

"You think it's something from her mom?" Cameron knew about the relationship I had with Jiao's mom and never judged me because the woman was older. She was actually very supportive and asked me on a few occasions, if I ever wanted to find out who killed her.

"Probably."

"Ok then. Call me when you leave. Its six now and I have another hour. If I don't hear from you, stop by if it's not too late."

"I want to see you. I'm sending you his address. I'll have Dreek ask Jiao to make some food and we can all have dinner."

"I don't feel like arguing with your ignorant ass brother tonight."

"Do it for me."

"Ughhhhh. Fine, but I'm coming in my work clothes."

"You can come naked and I'll still be right here waiting."

"You nasty. I'll see you in a few." I hung up with a smile on my face.

Cameron is a few years younger than me but I appreciated the hell out of her. She cooked dinner for me quite a few times and her sex is off the chain. The only person who has ever had me strung out is Jiao's mom but Cameron was doing a good job handling the position. I loved the way she said my name and I admit, I said hers a few times too.

I parked outside my brother's house and prepared myself for whatever she wanted to give me. Did I want it is the real question? I knocked on the door and the nanny opened it. I walked in the living room and Jiao was lying on Dreek's lap and he was on the phone. He pointed to a box and told me to look in it. Jiao hopped off the couch before I could get to it and took a piece of paper out. She handed it to me and had me read it.

"Where did you get this?"

"My dad's house."

"How did he not find it?" She started telling me how she went there and found things she didn't know were there, as well as what her father had been doing to her mom.

"Follow me Bash and can you carry the box with you?" I picked it up and went behind her. She opened a door to some room and told me to take all the time I needed.

"What's this?" I asked when she was on her way out the door.

"Bash, I didn't read everything but what I did read, I'm sure you would want to see. The ones that have your name in it, I'll let you have but I would like to read them first to make sure I didn't miss anything."

"Why are you doing this? You know I was having an affair with your mom."

"I didn't know my dad had infidelities prior to you two. Plus, my mom was in love with you." I smiled when she said it.

"Oh Jiao." She was about to close the door.

"Yea."

"Cameron is coming over, is that ok?"

"Cameron. Jaime's sister."

"Yea."

"What's that about?" She stood there grinning.

"We've been messing around for a minute now. We haven't told anyone because it's still fresh."

"I'm telling Dreek."

"Wait!" She shut the door and ran out. I laughed at how childish she was. I opened a book and read.

August 30, 2013

Bash and I had sex for the first time. I was nervous and couldn't stop shaking. I hadn't been with another man in years and didn't know if I could please him. What if I was too old? What if his dick was too big? So many thoughts ran through my head and I tried to back out a few times. He told me it was ok and calmed me down and the sex was perfect. The way Bash made love to every part of my body made me yearn for him every day after. Just thinking about him makes me weak." I smiled reading each entry. She wrote every day we were together and even about the vacations.

January 2, 2014

I came home early because I wasn't feeling well. I found out I was pregnant and knew right then, it was time to leave my husband. I knew the baby belonged to Bash because my husband and I hadn't slept together in months. I planned on telling him after I took a nap but never got the chance to because I came home and my husband was standing at the door holding the diaries I wrote in. I knew he was going to kill me but instead he sat me down and claimed to understand why I cheated. He said his infidelities were the reason and he promised not to cheat again.

I agree to make it work but there was no way I could leave Bash. I had his child in my stomach and still had plans on telling him. Unfortunately, that very night my husband beat the child out of me, unbeknownst to him. I went to the emergency room and told them I was mugged. I needed to know if my child was gone, even though I knew. I stayed away from Bash for a week and told him I had the flu. It wasn't the truth though. I knew he would kill my husband if he saw what he did and I couldn't hurt Jiao, even though I was suffering.

January 11, 2014

Today I was going to see Bash. After not being in his presence for a week, I couldn't wait to see him. I called and told him I'd meet him at the room later. Most of the morning, I cleaned the house because I know after a session with Bash, I'd be extremely tired. My husband walked around the house with an attitude and even followed me around cleaning. He was up to something and right now I didn't care.

I got myself together and now it's time for me to go get my man. I'm seriously thinking about running away with Bash tonight. I don't think I can live here anymore knowing I don't love him. Well diary, I'm going to make love to my man. I'll be writing in you soon.

That was the last entry, which is the exact date of Candiance's murder. I put the books down and laid on the bed. What the fuck is Jiao's father up to and could he be the one who murdered her. He knew she was sleeping with me and my name is all through the books. It's not a lot of Bash's out here. I wonder if he found out we were supposed to meet up, got there first, shot her and tried to frame me? Not like I would do a day in jail but it's the principle.

"Hey babe. You ok." Cameron came in and sat next to me.

"When did you get here?"

"I've been here for a few hours. Jiao told me what you were doing so I left you alone."

"A few hours. What time is it?"

"After eleven."

"Damn. I've been in here that long?"

"Yup. Are you ok? I can tell you were crying or as men say, *your eyes were sweating.*" I cracked a smile.

"I'm good. I was just reading how she felt, the things she went through and the day of the murder; it was as if she knew her husband was up to something. I can't believe she was pregnant by me."

"Where's the baby?" I put my head down and explained what happened.

"I'm sorry Bash."

"Thanks. My gut is telling me, her husband killed her." I let her read the last entry and she covered her mouth.

"Babe, it sounds like he knew and waited for her to leave. I know she doesn't say it but if you read between the lines, you can put it together."

"Do me a favor and don't mention it to Jiao." Dreek said as he stood at the door. We didn't even realize anyone was there.

"Don't tell me what?"

"Nothing. He asked if he could fuck Cameron here and I told him yes but not to tell you." Cameron threw a pillow at him.

"There's a room downstairs all the way in the back. Do you, but I don't want to hear no screaming, so please make sure the door is shut and music is on." She walked out.

"Why don't you want her to know?" Cameron asked.

"Because I'm going to make sure Bash kills him." I nodded and he left the room.

"Baby, I would never tell you not to handle your business. I know what y'all are about. All I'm going to say is be careful." She cupped my face and kissed me.

"Let me make love to you downstairs, all the way in the back with the doors closed and music up." We both started laughing.

"Not at all. I have to go home and shower first. You know we go for hours off and on. I'm dirty from work and I would like my man to shower with me. I think he knows why."

"I damn sure do. Let's go."

"Don't forget the book." Cameron reminded me and I only took the one with the last entry on it. I don't know if Jiao would notice but I'm going to take heed to what Dreek said. If she finds out, she'll probably go after him so it's better this way. Because if he did kill Candiance, his ass is mine.

Dreek

"So, you and Jiao are finally a couple." Jaime asked and passed me the Ace of Spades. We were celebrating Percy being engaged and actually staying that way. The last time he proposed, Sommer's ex came and ruined it.

"Yea. Shorty got me to settle down."

"WHATTTTT?" All of them screamed out.

"Shut the fuck up y'all." I took a sip.

"Who would've known a chick could get you to stop slinging dick? I swear, I thought we were going to have to sign you up for the sex addict class."

"Jaime, you better stop fucking with me." I threw one of the red cups at him and we all started laughing.

"We need to handle the issue at the warehouse, ASAP." Percy said reminding me of who was and has been there for a few months now.

"Tomorrow." He nodded. I wasn't about to worry about shit tonight but drinking and going home and fuck the shit out of my girl. Damn, it even sounds crazy, saying it.

The remainder of the night seemed to be going fine. I noticed the club becoming more packed and it was already after 1am. Usually, it doesn't concern me but with the number of guys walking in, I made sure to put everyone on alert.

Jaime stood up and I could see him shaking his head as someone came over to the VIP section. I followed his gaze and it was dumb ass Mandy. I guess she didn't get enough of my girl fucking her up.

She asked security if she could come in and I told them to let her through. I wanted to hear whatever it is she had to say. None of my boys left and I think it's because they all loved Jiao and wasn't about to let me make a mistake.

It's crazy though, because Mandy had on a dress almost similar to the first night she approached me and her hair was cut short. However, the fuck me heels, beat face and her pussy almost showing, did nothing for me. Call me sprung all you want, but this love shit is serious.

"What up Mandy?" I asked and the bitch had the nerve to take my drink out my hand and put it to her lips. J told me I can't put my hands on bitches anymore unless they hit me first but Mandy is trying the fuck out of me.

"I wanted to know why we haven't hooked up anymore." She handed me the cup and I smacked the shit out her hand.

"Still mean as hell."

"I'm going to ask you one more time before I throw your ass out of here." She tried to sit on my lap in a straddling position and I pushed her ass off. What the fuck is she on? I don't need anyone running back telling Jiao anything.

"Are you really acting like this over my ex best friend?" Now I was confused. She knew damn well I gave zero fucks about the bitch in her house who sucked my dick.

"Bye Mandy."

"I'm saying Dreek. Jiao ain't who she claims to be."

"What?"

"Jiao and I used to be best friends. I know all her secrets and you're going to find out soon enough. You were a pawn in her game."

"I'm not even about to sit here and listen to your hating ass." I stood up and so did she.

"I'm going to say this and leave because it's obvious, she can do no wrong." Me and my boys were now waiting for her to say it.

"Remember the night she met you and shot up the car, along with the people inside?"

"Yea. Why?"

"Have you ever asked her why she did it? What made her go out there and kill them?" She smirked. I snatched the bitch up by the throat.

"What the fuck are you saying?" Percy told me I needed to release her if I wanted to hear.

"Jiao, is not who she says she is and you didn't meet by coincidence."

"Yes, the fuck we did." Now I was confused and pissed.

"I'll let you think that but what you should do is go home and ask who her ex-boyfriend is and when's the last time she spoke to him." She winked.

"She doesn't have an ex-boyfriend."

"Oh, I see she ran that virgin line on you too." She threw her head back laughing.

"If I were you, I'd make sure the kid she had is yours too." She blew me a kiss and hauled ass. I tried to run after her but the guys blocked me in. I started tossing shit over in VIP.

"Yo, calm down Dreek. You know how petty she is. You can't believe anything she says." Jaime said.

"I'm killing Jiao if she lied to me." I pushed past them and went to use the bathroom. As I was in there, all I could think of was the shit Mandy said. Is she telling the truth or trying to get me to leave J? I never did ask Jiao about the shoot out and who the fuck is her ex-boyfriend? I pulled my clothes up, washed my hands and opened the door.

"Bitch, get that small ass gun out my face." I smacked the shit out of her and looked down at my phone going off.

Queenie: *I'm in labor. Are you coming up here?"* I went to respond and felt a pain in my shoulder. I looked up and this stupid bitch had the nerve to be grinning. She has to be the dumbest bitch I know. Who shoots someone and stands there?

264

"You know you're dead, right?"

"Not before I kill you." She shot me again in the leg.

This is the stupid shit I'm talking about. If I'm threatening to kill you, it won't be in the leg or arm. *Fucking amateurs.* My phone went off again and this time it was J. I put it in my pocket and pretended the two shots weren't hurting. I grabbed her by the neck and felt another burning sensation in my groin area. I hit the ground this time and all I could think of is, if she shot my dick off.

"Jiao, is next." She said and ran off. I laid on the ground desperately trying to retrieve my phone again.

"YO, WHAT THE FUCK?" I heard Robert yell.

"Do not call Jiao." I said loud enough for him to hear. The next thing I know, the lights came on and I passed out.

****

"Welcome back Mr. Puryear." I heard a guy say as held some flashlight shit in my eye.

"What happened?" I snatched the shit out my arm and tried to stand.

"Sir, you have to calm down." I snatched the doctor up by his collar.

"What happened to me?"

"Sir, you were shot but you're going to be fine. The one in your shoulder and leg required surgery and the one in your groin only grazed you. It may have felt worse than it was but there's no damage. I grabbed my dick and then tossed the cover to look at it. There was a bandage on the side but nothing big.

"What time is it?"

"8:00 in the morning. Your friend said he would be right back." As he said it Percy strolled in with breakfast.

"Good, you're up. Who did this to you?" The doctor continued to check me out. I never responded.

"Where did you tell Jiao I was?"

"I told her and Sommer we had to leave town ASAP. Of course, she asked why didn't you call or text her. I told her you would later. What the fuck is going on?

"I don't know but I'm about to find out." I unhooked myself from the machines and started putting my clothes on.

266

The nurse came running in when the monitors went berserk. I told her to get my discharge papers ready because I'm out. After ten minutes, she returned with the papers and medications.

"Oh shit. Queenie was in labor last night. Let me go check on her and see if she delivered. I need to get the kid testing right away." He followed me to the floor women give birth on and the nurse directed me to her room.

"You can't mention this to Dreek." I heard as I stepped inside.

"Can't tell me what?" She didn't answer and the further I walked in the room, the angrier I got.

"You better tell me right now, why the fuck you're holding my supposedly daughter." I held the gun to Marcus head. I only knew she was a girl from the little pink hat n. He had the nerve to smirk, so I hit him over the head repeatedly with the but of my gun. I didn't give a fuck he had a baby in his hands. I could hear the baby crying but I kept hitting him.

"Oh my God Dreek! STOP! My baby." She screamed out and it took me out my trance. Blood was everywhere and the baby stopped crying. I walked out the hospital room with no regrets.

Jiao

"Who do he think he is not calling me? Where could he be? I mean we weren't arguing or anything so I don't understand." I paced back and forth talking on the phone to Sommer.

"Sis, calm down. You're getting worked up and it's probably something to with their business in Cuba." I thought about what she said and I remember Dreek saying sometimes they would up and leave the country with no notice.

"Fuck this. I'm going to look for him."

"Where are you going to look fool? You have no idea where to even start."

"Bitch, I'm going to Queenie's and try to figure out where the bitch Mandy lives. I swear if he's over either of their house, I'm fucking killing him."

"Bring my nephew here before you go off and do something stupid."

"His nana is here and she just put him down for a nap. I'll call you when I hear something.

"Bitch, come get me then."

"Who's going to keep an eye on Raven?"

"The nanny. I'll be ready when you get here."

I hung up, ran in my room and threw on a sweat suit. I laced up my brand new peach and white air macs, grabbed my keys, phone and ran down the steps. I looked in the living room and Dree was lying on the couch watching cartoons as usual.

I thought about going in the room we had for Dreek's mom here and check on my son, but then she'll question the shit out of me. I don't need to hear her tell me not to lay hands on him either. I could never agree to it anyway; especially if he is with another chick.

I blew the horn in front of Sommer's house and she came out wearing an all black sweat suit with all black sneakers. At first, I was going to question her but changed my mind because she's my ride or die, so she's supposed to be

269

ready for war. She put her finger up when she got in the truck and told me to be quiet. It sounded like she was talking to Percy.

I took the hour drive over to Queenie's and scanned the parking lot. I was mad as hell because Dreek had us living far away and now it would take me longer to find him.

I had Sommer call her dad and ask if he could find Mandy's information out. At first, he said no, but then she called Susie, who called us back and gave it to us. She said Sommer's dad made her promise he could spend time with her if he gave it to her. Susie planned on taking him back once she found out the truth about Charlotte but said he had to suffer first.

"Pull over J." Sommer pointed to a gas station.

"For what? My tank is good."

"Charlotte is there and I want to see who she's with." She pointed again and sure enough, Charlotte came out the store and walked to a car with tinted windows.

"Follow the car." I snapped my neck.

"Bitch, Dreek ain't going nowhere." I sucked my teeth and did like she asked. The car drove to the projects and stopped. Both doors opened and you wouldn't believe who the fuck stepped out with her.

"What you want to do?"

"Let's find Dreek and we'll come back here another time."

"Sommer, I think we should deal with this now. What if they're not around when we return?"

"Oh, they'll be around. If they wanted to run, they would have. There's something here they want, and neither of them will leave town until they have it. We just have to figure out what it is." I pulled off and we were in route to my old best friends house.

"Bitch, there's no cars in the driveway. You think Mandy is here?" Sommer asked when we stepped out the truck.

"I need to make sure."

"OPEN THIS DOOR BITCH." I yelled out as I banged on it. I didn't care who the fuck heard me.

"DREEK, I SWEAR TO GOD IF YOU'RE IN THERE YOU BETTER SAY GOODBYE TO YOUR KIDS. I PROMISE YOU, I HAVE A BULLET FOR YOU." The more I yelled, the angrier I got. No one came to the door, so I kicked a window out and climbed in. Call me crazy all you want but a bitch had to be 100 percent sure he wasn't in here.

I opened the door for Sommer and made my way around Mandy's place. She had a decent spot and it the decorating wasn't bad. There was a unique smell in here, and only one person I know wears this type of cologne and it damn sure isn't Dreek. *When the fuck did he come here and is he looking for me?* I felt myself trembling and before I could turn the knob to the other bedroom, Sommer asked if I were ok. Instead of going in, I turned around and told her we had to leave.

"He's here."

"Who?" I raised my eyebrows.

"Bitch, I don't know what that means. Who the fuck is here because Dreek damn sure ain't?" I ignored her. I forgot no one knew about him, not even her. In due time, I will find that motherfucker but right now, my focus is on my so called man.

"Where else could they be? Didn't you say they had a warehouse?"

"Oh shit, that's right. I was so into following Charlotte I forgot to tell you. When Percy and I were talking, I heard Dreek in the background saying he had to put in some new orders before they get on the plane. They have to be there and if not, then they just left to go to Cuba."

"Orders. What the hell is that about?"

"I don't know but it's time to find out what Charlotte said Percy had hiding in the warehouse anyway." I forgot Charlotte's messy ass said that to her. We pulled on the dark street where the warehouse was and stepped out the car. It was quiet as hell out and all you could hear were crickets.

"Hello Jiao." I froze when I heard his voice. Sommer looked at him and then gave me a confusing stare. Why the fuck didn't we check our surroundings first?

"Long time no see baby." He licked his lips.

"The baby did your body real, real good." My phone started ringing and it was my father. I sent him to voicemail but couldn't help but wonder why he was calling me this late.

"Didn't think I'd see you two bitches here." Mandy said as she stepped out the car. Here we are down the street from my man's warehouse dealing with two people I'd rather not be around.

"Bitch. I don't think the last ass whooping was enough. Shall we go again." I put my hair up.

"I miss you baby girl." He kissed my neck and I smacked the shit out of him.

"Is that the way to treat the man who's going to kill your son's father and whisk you away to live the good life?"

"What do you want?" I stood there staring at him. Mandy had a big ass grin on her face.

"Who I want is standing behind you?" I turned around and there stood Dreek, Percy, Jaime, Robert and a shitload of other niggas. Dreek looked as if he were injured but I couldn't be certain. I did see what looks like a bandage under his shirt and the more he walked up on me, I noticed a slight limp.

"Somebody better tell me right now how you two know each other." The anger spoke volumes in Dreek's voice.

"Your baby daddy is going to kill you." Mandy pointed to my shirt. There sat a red dot on my chest. Sommer moved me out the way but the dot was everywhere I was. Why wasn't there a red dot on Sommer? Was he watching us from inside?

"Do you want to tell him my love, or should I?" He had a smug grin on his face.

"Oooh, let me tell it." Mandy said jumping up and down like a fucking kid.

"Dreek, this is my cousin Hector and you see." She walked up to me and stood in my face.

"Hector and Jiao were a couple a few years back and remember when I told you your precious Jiao wasn't what she seemed? Well, here you have it." She rubbed her hands together like she was delivering some important news.

"Meet the chick who was working with Hector to take down you down." Sommer looked at me and covered her mouth and I could feel everyone's eyes on me, but the only

275

ones mine met, were Dreek's. I saw love, sadness, hatred and most of all anger.

"Jiao no." Sommer said and Percy snatched her away from me.

"I can't save you J. You fucked up big time." Jaime said and moved past me.

"Dreek." He never said a word, which is worse than cursing me out.

"TAKE EM ALL OUT." Dreek said in his earpiece. He looked at me and walked away. I tried to run after him but shots rang out and it was a war zone.

To Be Continued...

CPSIA information can be obtained
at www.ICGtesting.com
Printed in the USA
LVHW02s1518270618
582082LV00014B/949/P

9 781976 581922